The Santa Suit

Christopher Brian Halvorson

BLACK RHINO PRESS
WWW.BLACKRHINOPRESS.COM

While no song lyrics are used in this novel, the author references the
following titles and performers:

"Merry Christmas Baby" Words and Music by Lou Baxter and Johnny Moore
Performed by Elvis Presley. RCA/Sony/BMG

"Little Saint Nick" Words and Music by Brian Wilson and Michael E. Love
Performed by the Beach Boys. EMI/Capitol Records

"The Man With All The Toys" Words and Music by Brian Wilson and Michael E. Love
Performed by the Beach Boys. EMI/Capitol Records

"Are You Lonesome Tonight" Words and Music by Lou Handman and Roy Turk
The Elvis Presley recording of this song bears the RCA/Sony/BMG label

"I Want You, I Need You, I Love You" Words and Music by Maurice Mysels and Ira Kosloff
The Elvis Presley recording of this song bears the RCA/Sony/BMG label

Cover layout by Jessica Cowden. Cover wreath design by Angela Dawn Perry

Halvorson, Christopher Brian, 1968–
The Santa Suit / Christopher Halvorson—First Edition

1. Product Liability Lawsuits—Santa—Fiction. 2. New York (N.Y.) Fiction.
3. Publicity campaign—Fiction. 4. Family resolutions—Fiction

ISBN 13: 978-0-9762238-1-8
ISBN 10:   0-9762238-1-3

Printed and published in the United States of America

BLACK RHINO PRESS
WWW.BLACKRHINOPRESS.COM
GRAND JUNCTION, COLORADO

dedicated to all of my readers,

especially my sister Nikki, the last in my
family to believe in Santa, and for all
those years she had to play "Elf"
beneath the Christmas tree.

acknowledgements

Special thanks to Roya Balali at *The Los Angeles Times* for her Persian cooking and unyielding optimism. Genius Girl Mireille at *Parade Magazine* for her careful edits while managing to police the streets of New York City for grammatical infractions. Producer Barrett Stuart for his interest and encouragement of the project (I'm still waiting for that introduction to Alison Eastwood by the way). Scott Erickson and family in Philadelphia; Jason and Rochelle Brooks on Planet O.C. The Alguards back home in Washington State (Christmas ham!) Dr. Steven Murray for introducing me to his doppelganger Howard Roark. Daniel Sullivan and Lynne Butler, mentors and writers, for their honest criticisms and praises over the years. The English and history faculties at the University of North Alabama, especially Dr. Foster, Dr. Gaunder, Dr. Riser, Dr. Smith and Dr. Price ("Crush the Infamous Thing!") and Dr. McDaniel ("Well, it's true....") Jacque Rainwater, former Miss UNA turned Miss Survivor (that day will bond us for life).

A toast to the MFA program at Columbia University, especially Janet Roach, whose "Roach's Rules" finally clarified the difference between form and formula. And to the people of New York City—I never realized how much I missed (or even liked) the Big Apple until writing this novel; and I'm pulling for the Mets though my characters are Yankees fans.

To my mother Judi (Jedi Judi Warrior), who broke every rule of her nature by letting me skip a day of school in fifth grade to watch the Sonics championship parade in downtown Seattle (the day a rebel was born). To brother Chuck, for teaching me how to force the opponent into dribbling on his weak side—a tactical strategy that works on and off the court (as much as I hate sports analogies). To my father Larry, for the free legal advice and possibly inspiring this story on a subconscious level; and to my sister Nikki, my future accountant if I ever have any real money to count. To Aunt Jackie and cousins Todd, Randy (and Tara); and to the loving memory of the Bee-Gees (not the disco group but my grandparents' pet nicknames for one another). Thanks to Val for her spicy pasta dinners—and Emma A. for her chocolate chip banana bread that fueled many late night writing sessions.

A heartfelt appreciation to producers Arthur Sarkissian, Adam Kline and Stephanie Striegel for opening their doors to a fledgling writer all those years ago; and to Phillip Rosen, entertainment lawyer extraordinaire and living proof there are decent people in showbiz. Hats off to Will Stubbs at Davis Entertainment for one small, yet enormous suggestion to the story (which wouldn't have worked otherwise).

And let's not forget Mrs. Evans and Mr. Okubo, retired veterans of Highlands Elementary. Ellie Garcia and her parrotfish Joy. And of course, Clem Edwards, infamous coach and fearless leader of HAB—the fightin' purple machine (and all who remain a part of it—especially the Leathleys, Fredelles, Rerecichs, and living memory of Ken Gerber, who is probably raising holy hell in Australia.)

PART ONE

~~DEAR SANTA~~

One

Had Henry Milton been looking outside the window of his third grade classroom, he would've seen there was no chance of a white Christmas that year. Rain clouds streaked the sky like angry graffiti over his Bronx neighborhood. Too busy at his desk to notice, Henry was writing a letter to Santa Claus.

"Remember, class," said his teacher Mrs. Collins. "Santa checks for grammar and spelling."

Henry felt his stomach tighten around the welfare corndog he'd ingested for lunch. *Dear Santa* he carefully spelled out. *All I want for Christmas is a Mr. Steely.* Beneath this request, he drew a picture of the battery operated robot that could march upstairs, swim in the bathtub, and even speak upon command in a digital voice. At least that's what the TV ad promised during Saturday morning cartoons. For Henry, it was love at first sight.

"Mister Steely, huh?" Mrs. Collins had suddenly cast a busty shadow over his desk.

"Yes, Mrs. Collins. I've been a very good boy this year."

"For a kid in this neighborhood, you're an angel."

Mrs. Collins was telling the truth. Since last Christmas, Henry had not ripped off a single thing, not even a comic book of *Camouflageman*, his favorite superhero made super by a radioactive chameleon bite.

Like his hero, Henry was able to disguise himself in the background of trouble. Never once did he pick his nose or fart in class like Frank Mulligan seated in front of him. Nor did he launch a single paper airplane during that boring film on the dangers of smoking; and when some curious brats immediately lit up in the boys' room after school, Henry turned down what would've been his first cigarette.

While avoiding such troubles, Henry religiously did his homework and volunteered to clean the boards for Mrs. Collins on days she wasn't feeling well, which was mysteriously at the beginning of every month. A true gentleman, he never even peeked down her blouse when she leaned over his desk, as she was doing now.

Breasts, like graffiti, could wait until puberty. All Henry wanted was Mr. Steely, and he had complete faith in Santa bringing him one.

If only he'd looked out that window.

Two

Early Christmas morning, the Miltons' shabby apartment was fairly quiet for the Bronx. The only sounds were a distant car alarm, a honking horn or two, and someone shouting "Yo!" Such noises were as common as waves lapping the shore in calmer places of the world, something Henry wouldn't know about as he came stampeding downstairs, disrupting whatever remained of that so-called quiet.

Still in pajamas, he made a beeline to the fireplace where his stocking bulged from Santa's visit. Tearing through it, he showered the air with Hershey's kisses, a cheap harmonica, packs of baseball cards, a plastic wristwatch—all those crappy fillers a boy has to go through to reach the treasured prize. With the anxiety of a looting pirate, Henry dug deep for his beloved Mr. Steely. Soon they would be together. Boy and robot. Batteries included in this perfect match.

Heart racing, Henry tipped the stocking upside down and shook it. A pair of dice tumbled onto the dingy carpet . . . a stale fortune cookie . . . a rubber eraser that caromed off his shin. But no Mr. Steely.

Dejected beyond belief, Henry peered into the dark, empty stocking that left him feeling just that: dark and empty. A monstrous pain arose in his chest and unleashed itself in a horrific scream: "I HATE YOU SANTA, YOU FAT, LYING DIRTY BASTARD!"

The reverberations of his voice shook the walls like a passing subway train. Even in the Bronx, this was loud enough to awaken his parents, who suddenly appeared like ghosts in their tattered white robes and pale morning faces.

Mr. Milton nervously cleared his throat. "Son, there's something we need to tell you. Santa Claus is not a fat, lying, dirty bastard." With a nudging elbow from Mrs. Milton, he confessed: "I'm the fat, lying, dirty bastard for losing my job at the plant."

Mrs. Milton nodded in agreement. "Sorry sweetie. We simply couldn't afford a Mr. Steely."

"And your mother wouldn't let me rip one off."

"Maybe for your birthday," she said, with another elbow to Henry's father.

Henry gazed up at his parents through teary eyes. "You mean, there is no Santa?"

His mother sadly shook her head no.

His overweight father strained to bend over for a Hershey's kiss, breaking wind in the effort. "The truth often hurts, kid. But this is the best we could do." Before he could unwrap the chocolate from its shiny foil, it was slapped away by a maternal hand.

But the hardest slap in the room was felt by Henry. Stung by reality, he tried imagining a world without Santa, one in which his father was a cheap substitute, a guy who spent most of his time at the bowling alley, guzzling beer and betting away his unemployment checks before stumbling home for leftover Hamburger Helper, most often without the hamburger.

No, no, no. Surely this must be a bad dream. Soon Henry would awaken and come charging downstairs to find Mr. Steely awaiting him.

A rumble of thunder outside jerked him back to reality once more. Henry watched raindrops pound the window like angry teardrops streaming down his face.

Merry Freakin' Christmas, New York.

Three

HAPPY NEW YEAR'S! appeared on the board in Mrs. Collins' class, a board that Henry would never volunteer to clean again. When he returned to third grade after Christmas break, Henry was a new man. At least that's what he considered himself, since he knew far more about the adult world than all these little saps seated around him. Foolishly they chattered away, bragging and showing off the goodies Santa had brought them. If only they knew the truth, suckers.

Mrs. Collins came slinking into the classroom in new vogue apparel. For the first time ever, Henry noticed his teacher was a *woman,* a very attractive woman, which probably explained her gold bracelet and suntanned face. Most likely, a rich husband had taken her to Hawaii and spoiled her with fancy presents. Too bad his mother wasn't pretty like her.

"Did everyone have a good Christmas?" she asked with a smile made brighter by her tan.

Everyone but Henry eagerly responded.

"Santa gave me this jersey!" Frank Mulligan wiped his snotty finger on Yankee pinstripes.

"Santa gave me a Barbie!" Amy Gibson waved her doll to show off their matching hairdo and outfit.

"Santa gave me a Mr. Steely!" Jimmy Calhoun wound up his shiny new robot and sent him marching across his desk.

Henry couldn't bear to watch, but did so anyway. Like the time an old lady fell onto the subway tracks right before the train came—only this time he was the one getting slammed.

"Santa brought me a make-up kit!" Vicky Mills put lipstick on her smile and batted mascara lashes. "And my mom says I'm old enough to wear it."

"That's because your mom *is* Santa Claus, you stupid hussy."

The entire class turned to Henry with a horrified gasp.

"Henry Milton! What has gotten into you?"

"You lied to us, Mrs. Collins, 'cause there is no Santa."

"Don't listen to him, class. Henry is just upset."

"Yeah, well if Santa Claus is real, then why does Boogers have a store tag on his jersey?" Reaching for Frank seated in front of him, Henry ripped the tag off the back of his Yankee pinstripes. "Looks like your mom paid $99.99 at the Locker Room. Tell 'er she got ripped off."

A dumbstruck silence fell over the room until Amy Gibson burst into tears, desperately clutching her Barbie twin. That started a wave of sobs to ripple across the class.

Mrs. Collins stood helplessly before them. Never did she appear so disappointed in one of her students. "Shame on you, Henry. I'll be seeing you after school."

"You can't punish me for telling the truth." Henry defiantly opened his social studies book to see a photo of a starving kid in Africa. Nothing was fair in this world, and nobody would ever fool him again.

Four

From that day on, Henry would submerse himself in books. But he wasn't looking for an escape from reality like the kids reading about dragon slayers or youth detectives or sports legends. No sir, Henry was focused on learning. Though he wasn't sure what he wanted to be someday, he knew one thing for sure: He didn't want to grow up to become his father, a guy who barely skimmed the sports section for spreads on betting games.

The years passed by surprisingly fast to Henry's satisfaction. He grew taller and more handsome. His blond hair turned a sandy brown. Amazingly, his eyes turned a darker shade of blue, like oceans polluted with too much information about world problems. While Henry excelled in every subject in school, he definitely gravitated toward the social sciences. Not that he believed in society, but he did believe in stories of individuals fighting for justice: Modern day battles that resonated of David and Goliath, only in courtrooms and legislation buildings instead of bloody war fields.

Therefore, it was no surprise that Henry chose law school at City U. after finishing a degree in history at the same institution. Sure, it wasn't Harvard or Yale, but he was proud to be coming off the streets, armed with the same knowledge as his future Ivy League opponents. Only Henry was harder, tougher, hungrier.

What Henry didn't realize was that he was writing his own version of those fairy tales he so despised. Like Jack climbing the beanstalk, he was always looking up, always rising, always hoping for a match with that giant in the clouds.

Perhaps that is why he became a products liability specialist—from jock itch sprays causing allergic reactions, to soup cans poisoned with botulism, to sunglasses lacking UV protection. Regardless of the damage, Henry was sure to make the corporations pay. While fighting for the everyman, he managed to collect a few golden eggs for himself, though he was far from rich.

What Henry really needed was a big case, the kind you see for weeks on cable TV news, the kind that would secure a future for his wife and son (who should've been mentioned before his career). So busy looking ahead, Henry forgot about their needs at home. Not long after his thirty-fifth birthday, his wife Trish asked for a divorce, one of the few requests he could manage. They agreed their eight-year-old son Junior would stay with Mom, but Henry was welcome, if not encouraged, to see their boy whenever he wished.

If Henry would only stop to pull his head out of the clouds, he might've realized that Junior was now the same age as when he discovered the truth about Santa Claus.

Or fraud, depending on how you looked at it.

Five

Thanksgiving was Henry's day to spend with Junior. What better way to spend it than at the Macy's Parade, among the thousands of people cramming the sidewalk for a glimpse of a passing float. Had Henry been a normal spectator, he might've seen a thirty-foot turkey approaching, but he was busy hunting clients, not birds, in the crowd.

Some clown in a Red Sox cap was about to sip from a can of diet cola. Henry rushed over with his *Attorney at Law* card. "Just in case that metal tab rips off and you swallow it."

Mr. Sox took a painful gulp of fizz.

"Internal bleeding," warned Henry. "It could happen ya know."

"You some kind of doctor?"

"Jurist doctor."

"Should've known." Mr. Sox checked to make sure the tab was on before taking another sip.

"Call me if you get brain cancer. Artificial sweeteners have been link-ed to—"

"Get lost," said Mr. Sox with a fizzy belch.

"Yeah, you're welcome." Henry took off into the crowd to rescue his next potential client.

"Dad! Wait up!" Junior plowed through much larger bodies to catch up to his father. Glasses steamed, he donned a Yankees cap and jacket that Henry had gotten him for his birthday. A camera swung from his neck-band. "I wanna get a picture of Santa!"

Henry shuddered. "Aren't you getting a little old for that stuff?"

"Mom says there's a Santa. And here he comes!" Junior stood on tiptoes for a peek through the cheering crowd.

"That's just some poor slob in a red suit."

"I know. Like the guy at the mall with the ice cream stains on his beard. Mom says he's fillin' in for the real Santa, 'cause he can't be every-where at once."

"There is no Santa. Period."

"How can you prove it?"

"Listen, son. The only things living in the North Pole are Eskimos and penguins."

"I thought penguins lived in the South Pole?"

"Geography was never my specialty."

"We actually studied that in science, Dad."

"North Pole or South Pole, there is no Santa." Case closed, Henry nudged his way to a pair of boys sucking helium out of balloons. "Hey! Did those come with a warning?"

The boys, most likely brothers with identical green eyes, responded in high squeaky voices: "No way, man. Why should they?"

"Because helium can cut off the oxygen to your brain."

The boys' mother whirled in alarm. "You're kidding?"

"No ma'am. Might hurt their sales if parents knew their kids could die or end up like vegetables."

Horrified, the mother watched her boys inhale off the shrinking balloons. "Stop that right now!"

The boys giggled and staggered around. "Chill out, Mom," they said in voices sounding like the munchkins in *Wizard of Oz.*

Junior laughed at their performance. "Can I have a balloon, Dad?"

"No. This isn't a laughing matter." Henry handed his card to the panicked mother. "Just in case something tragic happens." With a grim face, he led Junior away.

"Dad! You scared that poor lady!"

"I simply informed her of something she needs to be aware of."

"But still—"

"I may have saved those kids from a future of drooling on themselves."

"What about me, Dad? Today was supposed to be our day—before you dump me off at Mom's house."

"I don't *dump* you off. I *drop* you off."

"That's not what Mom says. I heard her talking on the phone to Aunt Reggie."

"Your mom says *tomatoes.* And I say *ta-mah-toes.*"

"Is that why you're getting divorced? Because you disagree on everything?"

"That might have something to do with it. But there is one thing we agree on."

"What's that?"

"That we have the coolest kid in America."

Junior smiled brightly. "You really think so?"

"I know so. But don't get a big head or your cap won't fit." Henry pulled the bill over Junior's eyes and darted ahead. Right in front of them was a big brute about to chomp into a hot dog. "Sir! Are you aware that hot dogs are the leading cause of fatal choking?"

Shocked to hear this, the brute choked on his wiener. Eyes widening in terror, he grasped his throat for help.

"Dad! Look what you did!"

"Nice to meet you," said Henry, wrapping the guy in a bear hug from behind. "I'm Henry Milton, and before I perform the Heimlich maneuver, I will need your consent."

The brute frantically nodded.

"I'll accept your nodding as a waiver of liability. As your legal advisor, I strongly recommend you seek damages from those greedy hot dog manufacturers. Their tubular design can easily lodge in the throats of—"

"Dad! His face is turning blue!"

"Okay, Junior! Take a picture!" Henry posed with a smile next to his choking victim. Junior reluctantly took aim with his camera and snapped the photo. In a flash, Henry thrust his fists into the brute's abdomen and lifted him off his feet. Surprised by his own strength, he yanked him up and down as a human rag doll. Finally came a loud pop with the force of an opening champagne bottle. Instead of a cork was a flying chunk of wiener.

The crowd applauded. After a quick bow, Henry handed the brute his card. "Don't thank me for saving your life or anything. Though a phone call would be nice."

The brute nodded uncertainly while wheezing to catch his breath.

Before he could say no, Henry stole his napkin and quickly gathered the stray piece of hot dog. "Come on, Junior. We got all the evidence we need." Snatching the photo, he led his son away.

Junior shook his head in dismay. "All I wanted was a picture of Santa."

Six

The front steps of the apartment building were like a time vacuum, each broken slab of concrete sucking Henry into his past.

"Hey Dad! Wanna come in?" Junior scrambled toward the graffiti-covered entrance that lacked a doorman. "You can see our Christmas tree. I made the star on top myself."

"I'd love to see it, hotshot, but maybe another time." Henry looked uneasily at a third story window that flew open.

Trish Milton stuck her face out. More cute than pretty, she wore her hair in a ponytail that was peppered with wood shavings. Likely interrupted from one of her sculptures, she called down in a Bronx accent: "Don't tell me! Parade ended early this year?" She accusingly tapped her watch.

Henry shrugged and smiled. "Hey Trish. Didn't want you to worry."

Trish gave him a skeptical look before smiling at their son with the camera around his neck. "Hey sweetie! D'you get your picture of Santa?"

"No. Dad says there is no Santa."

"Don't listen to 'em, Junior. He doesn't know what he's talkin' 'bout."

"Oh yes I do! That 'Saint' Nick will only break your heart, once you realize he's a big fat fraud."

"But Dad? If Santa's not real, why do you hate him so much?"

"Because your father's on his naughty list."

"I am not!" Henry kneeled before his son. "Listen, Junior. You can't depend on Santa for presents. That's what your dad is for, and that's why I'm working my tail off to get you anything you want."

"Anything?"

"Well, besides a Ferrari, or owning the Yankees, or a diamond necklace for your mother, even though she would look stunning in it."

Trish touched her neck with a smile. "You never bought me one when we were together, so why should you now?"

Henry glanced away, already regretting the mild flirtation. Now Junior was looking hopefully at him and Trish together.

"Hey Dad. You know what I really want for Christmas?"

Henry prayed for a way out of this one. Miraculously, his cell phone rang in a Christmas jingle. *Tis the season to sue somebody, fa-la-la-la.* Winking at Junior, he flipped it on. "Henry Milton, attorney at—yes, yes, mm-hmm. Yes, this sounds like a winner. Okay! Meet me at my office in twenty minutes!"

Off he raced down the steps and into the street to flag a cab. Once safely buckled into the backseat, he gave a big thumbs up like an astronaut taking off on a mission. Had he thought to look in the rearview mirror, he would've seen his son gazing sadly at his vanishing act.

"Your father means well," Trish said from above. "He just doesn't get it."

Junior glumly nodded and retreated inside the apartment building.

The window closed behind them, a mother's words lost in the wind-blown exhaust of Henry's cab.

Seven

The dirty skyscraper rose high into the clouds, the perfect viewpoint for any giants happening to appear. Among the hundreds of dingy windows, only one light was on Thanksgiving Day. Of course that office belonged to

Henry as he awaited his golden goose. Seated at his desk, he frantically flipped through a book on "Safety Regulations for Toys."

Without knocking, a snooty mother marched her plump, bratty son in. His dragging footsteps alerted Henry to jump up and greet them. "You must be Mrs. Truffle. And you must be her handsome son Bradley."

Bradley silently licked off a lollypop. A rainbow of colors smeared his pouting moon face.

Mrs. Truffle gave him a little nudge. "Say hello, Bradley."

Bradley reluctantly spoke in a whistling voice: "Hey, Mr. Lawyer."

"Well, hello there! Sounds like someone has a magic elf whistle stuck in his throat?"

"My mom told you that on the phone."

"Nothing to be ashamed of, young man. Those toy manufacturers never should've designed a whistle that could be swallowed by children."

Mrs. Truffle stroked her son's messy hair. "My poor baby had a part lined up in a Broadway musical. Now his voice is ruined."

"I was gonna be a pirate in *Peter Pan*," whistled Bradley.

"I love pirates!" said Henry. "So tell me, who am I gonna sue?"

"Santa Claus gave me the whistle last Christmas."

Henry forced a smile at the pudgy boy. "Sure he did. Now lemme have a minute with your mom."

"What're ya gonna do to her?"

Henry raised his eyebrows at the prudish Mrs. Truffle. "We're just gonna talk, kid."

Bradley measured Henry up with a suspicious look. With a decisive lick on his lollypop, he finally waddled out with whistling breaths.

"Okay," said Henry, left alone with Mrs. Truffle. "Where'd you really buy the toy? Was there a warning on the box? A manufacturer's address? Any receipts or—"

"Weren't you listening to my son? Santa Claus gave it to him."

"You're joking, right?"

"No, I never put a magic elf whistle in Bradley's stocking."

"Maybe your husband did."

"He left me five years ago."

Henry nodded in complete understanding. "Were you having these episodes?"

"I'm not crazy, Mr. Milton!"

"And you don't look like someone hitting the crack pipe?"

"Never! I don't do drugs!"

"Well, they do have prescription medications, Mrs. Truff—"

"Bradley's doctor gave us all the evidence we need." From her handbag she produced an X-ray; it clearly revealed the whistle lodged in Bradley's throat. "See—it says 'Made in the North Pole' right here—"

Henry squinted at a tiny engraving on the whistle. "That's a marketing gimmick. Until you find out who the real toy manufacturer is, I can't take your case."

"But it was Santa Claus!"

Henry opened the door for her with a polite smile. "Have a Merry Christmas."

Mrs. Truffle snatched the X-ray and stormed out of his office. "Let's go, Bradley. This dim-witted lawyer doesn't know anything."

Henry closed the door behind her and locked it with a sigh.

From down the hallway came a whistling sob.

Eight

Henry was late again. Waiting for him somewhere inside the crowded Manhattan lounge was the woman he'd been dating a few months now. Still not sure if she was his girlfriend or not, Henry had yet to press the issue of defining their relationship.

What he did know about Nora Powers was the following: A former teen model, she had quickly figured out that even the beautiful people could be discarded just as quickly as the glossy pages they appeared on. In a business that required fresh new faces on rail figures, she had witnessed too many girls waste away on a cocaine diet, the perfect energizer that suppressed appetite. By the age of twenty, most of these former super teens had withered into mindless skeletons without diplomas or futures, something they never thought about in front of a camera, the perfect instrument for capturing the moment and nothing else.

But Nora was different. Able to see beyond the lens, she started making contacts in the advertising world. Offered a summer internship at a top New York firm, she quickly snatched it up while gaining twenty pounds between June and September of her senior year in high school. With her new figure, she had eliminated herself from modeling assignments; yet she looked far more mature with her womanly breasts and hips. To her surprise, people started taking her more seriously, which in turn, made her take herself more seriously.

Instead of college, she rose through the ranks of file clerk, receptionist and assistant until she was finally a junior executive. Voluptuous, beautiful and earning six-figures a year, she had what most women her age could only dream of. But that still wasn't enough for Nora Powers. Before she was old enough to meet a client for a drink, she shocked everyone at the firm by leaving to give birth. Her baby was the Nora Powers Advertising Agency, and like any nurturing mother, she dedicated her life to seeing it grow.

Now, just a few weeks after her twenty-first birthday, she was already making a name for herself. Aggressively seeking clients, she shared in Henry's drive to hustle, hustle, hustle. Perhaps that is why a woman like Nora Powers was interested in a guy like Henry.

"Sorry I'm late," he said, as he finally found her at the bar.

Nora barely glanced up from her sketchpad drawing. "You'd be fired by now in advertising," she said with a teasing smile.

"You can't fire a new boyfriend."

"You're still on probation, buster." Nora grabbed his tie and reeled him in for a kiss.

"Oh really? Well I think you're the one who's in trouble." Henry pointed to her drawing of a hunky male in jungle-striped briefs. Surrounded by a pack of sex-starved women, he held up a bottle of Tiger Cologne as if it were a trophy. In a spraying mist came the slogan read by Nora:

"One sniff and the ladies will pounce." She playfully dug her nails into Henry. "My clients are gonna love it. They know what sells, and it's not brains."

Henry chuckled. "At least your clients are sane. I just met with some lady who wants to sue Santa Claus."

"What on Earth for?"

"Her kid swallowed a magic elf whistle." Henry imitated Bradley's whistling voice: "And now he talks like this."

Nora laughed. "I think you should take it."

"Is it the holidays? Driving everyone batty?"

"Think about it, Henry. The media would eat this up."

"And I'd become the laughingstock of New York. Maybe the country."

"There's no such thing as bad publicity. Especially for a lawyer. Like you."

"I could never stoop this low."

"You chase complete strangers on the street."

"I don't 'chase' anyone. I'm hustling clients."

"With your face on every TV and newspaper in the country, you'd have all the free advertising you could ever wish for."

Henry considered the possibility. No way would *The New York Times* run his story and photo of saving the choking guy from the wiener. But maybe they'd go for something absurd like this. "Technically, it is possible to file a suit against anyone."

"Santa Claus named as a defendant in federal court. That's every reporter's dream."

"What would I put for his address? The North Pole?"

"Why not? Millions of kids send him letters each year."

"Yeah. I remember those days," Henry somberly agreed.

"Hey, we'll get a press photo of the naughty lawyer dropping 'The Santa Suit' in the mail."

"The Santa Suit," repeated Henry with a grin. "I like that. I'll have to pretend I'm surprised when he fails to appear in court."

"Better yet. A case you don't even have to prepare for."

"Sounds too good to be true. You really think we can pull this off?"

Nora smiled and raised her glass. "Call that crazy client back."

Henry took out his phone, ready for some free publicity. On the wall were autographed photos of Joe DiMaggio, Frank Sinatra, and John Lennon, the Beatle who once claimed to be more popular than the man whose birth started Christmas.

"Hello, Mrs. Truffle. After further consideration, I think you have a very solid case. . ."

PART TWO

WAR

One

A few days later, Junior and Trish shared the morning edition of the *Times* over bowls of bran cereal, despite the protests of Junior to have Lucky Charms. According to his mother, they were not a magical way to start the day, even if they were magically delicious, as the TV ads had proven to be telling the truth.

Gulping down the soggy flakes before he could taste them, Junior wondered if his father ate what he was supposed to as a growing boy. If not, that might explain something. "Hey Mom. Why was Dad on Santa's naughty list?"

"Oh, I'm sure there were lots of reasons," said Trish with her nose in the paper.

"Did he eat too many sweets? Spit in his teacher's coffee? Fart on kids in class? Push people off the swings? Torment animals? Swear at old people?"

"I really can't tell you, sweetie. Your dad never talks about his childhood." Trish turned the page and her eyes widened in surprise. "But he sure carries a grudge."

Junior curiously leaned over to see the headline: THE SANTA SUIT: SANTA SUED FOR UNSAFE TOY. A black-and-white photo showed his father posing with some bratty fat kid. Standing in front of a mailbox, they were about to drop off a lawsuit addressed to the North Pole.

"According to the boy's attorney," read Junior, "Santa Claus is clearly to blame for the magic elf whistle being swallowed."

Junior looked up in disbelief. "Dad is really suing Santa?"

"It sure looks that way," said his bewildered mother.

"How can you sue someone you don't even believe in?"

"I have no idea, honey. I think your dad could use some therapy."

Unable to eat another bite of soggy bran flakes, Junior pushed his bowl aside to read the rest of the article. Seeing his father's name several times, which happened to be the same as his, Henry Milton, Junior looked as if he might vomit on the kitchen table.

And his mother said Lucky Charms were an unhealthy way to start the day.

Two

It was miserably cold outside the federal superior courthouse in New York City. That might explain such a small gathering of reporters on the courthouse steps. Or maybe Henry Milton's lawsuit against Mr. Claus simply wasn't that big of a news story yet. After all, it was buried on page 23 of the *Times;* and though it faired better in the tabloids, readers were still more interested in Elvis sightings and UFOs than some half-baked lawyer picking a fight with Kris Kringle.

Among the reporters were Patrick Carol and Carol Patrick, hosts of the Action-7 News segment *From Both Angles.* Despite fierce winds, they both had perfect hair in place, their frozen smiles appearing as if they might crack with another drop in Fahrenheit.

"Joining you live from the courthouse as we await Santa's trial, I'm Patrick Carol."

"And I'm Carol Patrick, though few of us really expect Mr. Claus to appear today. What do you think, Patrick?"

"Oh, I'm putting my money on Santa, Carol."

"And so is Henry Milton, the lawyer suing him for ten million dollars on behalf of his client, Bradley Truffle."

"The boy who swallowed a magic elf whistle."

"And is now claiming the toy was hazardous."

"Due to its narrow tubular shape," said Patrick, with an expression that suggested he should've worn thermal underwear.

"According to federal safety regulations, a children's whistle should have a wider base to prevent choking."

"That's right, Carol, like the one we have here—" Patrick held up a whistle that was ridiculously oversized.

"Is that a whistle or a tuba, Patrick?"

"Why don't we let our viewers decide?" Patrick blew the hideous whistle that sounded like a foghorn.

Patrick and Carol chuckled with foggy breaths.

"Here he comes," said a voice from a competing network.

The huddle of reporters came to life like animated icicles, quickly getting cameras and microphones into place. Their main target was Henry as he led Nora and the Truffles up the steps.

Bradley, too pudgy to button his suit jacket, was licking off another giant lollypop. "You're lucky we took you back as our lawyer," he whistled in the wind.

"We're both lucky, kid," said Henry, eyeing the news cameras above. "But try and look like you're really hurting."

"That won't be hard with all these dumb steps." Already out of breath, Bradley glared at the hovering reporters.

"Hey Bradley! How can you prove the whistle came from Santa?"

"It was in my stocking, you idiot."

"Mrs. Truffle? Have you ever been treated for mental illness?"

"Stop calling me crazy!"

"Mr. Milton! You don't really believe in Santa, do you?"

"I don't *believe* in Santa, because he's putting unsafe toys in the hands of children."

Nora went prowling up the steps behind them, careful not to draw attention from Henry with her beauty. Smiling proudly in the background, she watched her campaign launch successfully. After all, nobody ever said the news couldn't be funny.

Three

Strangely enough, his father looked taller and wider on a twenty-inch TV screen. Even his voice sounded deeper through the speaker: "As the father of an eight-year-old, I shouldn't have to fear for my son's life. . ."

"Is Dad doing this for me?" Junior asked his mother seated on the couch beside him.

"Uh, yeah, that's it. No, wait, I can't lie to ya too. Your father's performing for the news cameras, and loving every minute of it."

Junior watched his father in disappointment. "He's gonna be sorry when Santa shows up in the courtroom."

"Well, sweetie," his mother nervously replied, "Don't be too surprised if Santa doesn't make it to New York."

"Why not?"

"Oh, I'm sure he's busy making toys. I mean, it is almost Christmas."

Junior gave his mother an inquisitive stare, which she quickly avoided by watching his father on TV. Sad but true, it was the only way the three of them could be in the same living room together.

Four

Courtroom 86F was normally used for criminal trials. On the eighth floor, it was less likely someone would try to escape out the window. Due to a flooding toilet on the third floor, it would be facilitating civil cases this afternoon.

Packed together were lawyers and their clients. Today's defendants wore Ralph Lauren instead of prison jumpsuits, their wrists in Rolex watches instead of handcuffs.

The absence of prosecutors and criminals meant nothing to Judge Thorne, who treated everyone younger than himself as an offender. Now in his late seventies, that was most people. A former naval commander, Judge Thorne had zero tolerance for outbursts, pranks, or wise-cracking lawyers. That might explain his sour expression as he heard Henry's complaint:

"Had the whistle been inspected at Santa's toy factory, my client could've been spared the pain, suffering, and humiliation—"

"And where is this factory located, Mr. Milton?"

"Why, the North Pole, your Honor. See, it says so right here on the whistle." Henry presented the X-ray from Bradley's doctor.

Judge Thorne snatched the photo and lifted his bifocals to closely examine the tiny engraving. "Made in the North Pole. Baloney."

"Then someone's in violation of Santa's copyright."

"Cut the crap, Milton. My docket's overfilled and you're holding up our judicial process."

"Actually, sir, it's Santa holding us up, since he's the one who's failed to appear."

"The federal taxpayers may not find your antics so funny."

"I would certainly hope not, your Honor. My client's suffering is nothing to laugh at." Henry gestured to his client in the front row. "Say hello, Bradley."

Bradley reluctantly stood with a nudge from his mother. Unsure what to do with his lollypop, he licked it once more before addressing Judge Thorne: "Hello," he whistled.

The audience laughed at the boy with a parrot's voice.

"Shut up!" chirped Bradley, hiding his face in his mother's arms.

"Thanks to Santa's faulty designs," said Henry sympathetically, "My client will live the rest of his life with a whistle in his throat."

Judge Thorne dryly responded: "I thought it was Santa's elves who designed the toys."

Rising laughter filled the courtroom.

Henry managed to keep a straight face. "Yes, your Honor, but Santa employs those elves, who are miniature agents of his—"

"Mr. Milton, are you familiar with Rule Eleven?"

"Mmm, something to do with frivolous lawsuits, which thankfully doesn't apply here."

"Rule Eleven means I can fine you, throw you in jail, and take away your law license. And right now I'm getting very close to—"

"Look!" said a little boy pointing outside. "It's Santa!"

Whoosh! Several reindeer whizzed past the row of windows in a blur of hooves and antlers and jingling bells. Behind them appeared Santa in his sleigh. With a crack of his whip, he raced by as quickly as he'd appeared.

A stunned silence hung over the courtroom. Nora staggered to her feet in hopes of another Santa spotting. Judge Thorne took off his glasses, batted his eyes, and put them back on again. Henry stood frozen, momentarily paralyzed from thought, speech or even breath. Bradley and Mrs. Truffle were the only ones who did not look surprised.

"That stupid Santa," whistled Bradley. "He'd better gimme my money."

The silence broken, an excited chatter made Judge Thorne's courtroom sound like a school cafeteria. "Order in the court," he weakly demanded with a shaky tap of his gavel. Former Naval Commander perhaps, but he had never piloted a reindeer-drawn sleigh, and now he was going crazy like those miscreants he usually held in contempt.

Five

Outside the courthouse, a crowd had quickly gathered to watch Santa buzzing through the clouds in crazy spirals. Was he trying to make a statement, like the wicked witch in Oz? Or was he simply having trouble with his reindeer? Perhaps he had never attempted a landing on the street before, as he was generally accustomed to quick stops on rooftops. Like a FedEx carrier, he came swiftly in the night, no signature required, I'll take my milk and cookies now, thank you.

"San-ta! San-ta! San-ta!" the crowd began to chant. Children looked thrilled by Santa's daredevil flight around skyscrapers and telephone poles. Their parents and grandparents looked even more delighted, as they now got to believe in something that was previously reserved for kids.

"Where's Rudolph?" asked a little girl.

"That's what I was wondering," replied her grandmother.

Had they taken a better look into the sky, they would've realized his glowing red nose wasn't needed on a clear, sunny day.

"Whoaaaaaa!" Santa called from above while trying to gain control of his reindeer. "Easy does it, Prancer! Or I'm gonna have to get ya neutered!" With a tug on the reins, Santa finally steered them into a nosedive for the courthouse. Like a drunken team of Alaskan sled dogs, they headed straight for the growing crowd of reporters below.

Whoosh! Hats flew off the ducking newsmen's heads. Miraculously, Patrick Carol and Carol Patrick kept their hair perfectly in place. For those wondering what hair products they used, now was not the time to ask. For they were busy directing their cameraman to capture every moment of Santa's flying circus.

"It appears that Santa's coming in for a landing!" Patrick shouted.

"As the crowd scatters out of the way!" reported Carol.

Yards away, the reindeer finally touched down on the street in a rowdy herd. "Whoooooaaaaaaa!" Santa pulled on the reins with all his might.

Leaning back in his seat, he finally brought them to a grinding halt. After a long journey, his reindeer slowly calmed down with steam rising from nostrils.

Still antsy was Prancer, rearing up to butt the air with his antlers.

"That's it, Prancer. You're going to the vet when we get back." Santa climbed out of his sleigh with a team of elf lawyers in suits and ties. Wearing round little spectacles, they carried briefcases made of the finest leather.

"Are those made of reindeer hide?" questioned an animal rights activist in the crowd.

"Gosh no," Santa replied. "Though Prancer had better watch out."

Escorted by his mini-entourage, Santa went marching up the courthouse steps. In the midst of his presence, the astounded reporters stepped aside to let him through. Speechless for the first time since laryngitis in grade school, Carol Patrick quickly got her voice back:

"Wake up, New York! Wake up, America! Wake up, World!"

"Santa Claus has arrived," Patrick Carol announced.

Six

Inside the courtroom, Henry watched the doors burst open like a scene in a spaghetti western. Barging in were Santa and his elf lawyers.

"Sorry I'm late, your Honor. Got caught in a storm over the Atlantic. That time of year."

Judge Thorne wearily looked at Santa. "Just who are you anyway?"

Santa flipped open the lawsuit addressed to the North Pole. "Santa Claus, but I'm also named as defendant."

The audience laughed.

Henry nervously chuckled with them.

Judge Thorne raised his voice: "I don't know how you pulled off that flying stunt out there, but you will not make a mockery of my courtroom."

"Of course not, Jimmy. You've always been a very good boy."

"That's 'Judge Thorne.' And how'd you know my name? Which is James by the way." Only his initials were revealed on his bronzed name-plate: *Honorable J.L. Thorne.*

"You were easy to remember," said Santa with a mysterious twinkle in his eye. "The only six-year-old boy who wanted a chocolate Easter bunny for Christmas."

"That was more than half a century ago," said Judge Thorne in surprise. "How'd you know that?"

"Because I'm the one who put that chocolate Easter bunny in your stocking, Jimmy, I mean James, I mean, Judge Thorne."

"Well, Mr. *Claus*, why don't you tell me what I got the next year?"

Santa nudged his lead elf lawyer, Mr. Elfsquire, who typed into a mini-laptop before reporting: "Second grade, you asked for a Barbie doll, which your father wouldn't let you keep."

Explosive laughter filled the courtroom.

Henry laughed the loudest.

"That was for my sister!" retorted Judge Thorne with burning red cheeks. "I wanted ice skates! To play hockey!"

"Of course you did," said Santa. "And that's what I brought you in the third grade."

"But a nasty winter flu kept our future Wayne Gretzky indoors," said Mr. Elfsquire, his monitor now showing Jimmy in bed with a shiny new pair of skates.

"And I quickly outgrew them before the pond froze again," recalled Judge Thorne with a strained memory. "Why didn't I ask for another pair?"

"Because you stopped believing in me in the fourth grade."

Judge Thorne blinked at Santa in acknowledgement. "Yes, and maybe it's time to remove myself from this bench." Slowly he rose with rickety knees.

"Not so fast, your Honor." Santa lumbered toward the bench in his sooty black boots. "I'm older than you and I'm not about to retire over some spoiled ingrate and his greedy lawyer."

Several little briefcases popped open. "We're ready for trial," declared Mr. Elfsquire. Collecting the elves' briefs, he presented them to Judge Thorne.

"Wait!" Henry protested. "I'm going to need an extension!"

Judge Thorne settled back into his bench to smile down on Henry. "You're lucky to have the rest of the day so I may review the defense's brief."

"Please your Honor! At least a week!"

"You filed this lawsuit, Milton. Trial will resume tomorrow at oh-nine-hundred hours."

Seven

Henry didn't even remember walking back to his seat in the courtroom. Dazed by the sudden turn of events, his past ten seconds had simply evaporated from the time-space continuum.

"Are you okay?" asked Nora seated beside him.

"Oh, I'm doing great. So much for your publicity stunt."

"Henry, you're about to become the most famous personality on TV."

"Yeah, as the lawyer who got his butt kicked by Santa."

"Oh, come on. He's using elves as his lawyers."

"Little man's complex. They always make the toughest opponents."

"Show some poise," said Nora. "Those reporters out there smell fear like bloodhounds."

Henry nervously gazed beyond the doors at the bastion of media cameras. "Let's hold a press conference to withdraw my suit." From his tattered briefcase, he removed a notepad. "Help me write something here." Scribbling away, he unwittingly drew the head and torso of a long forgotten robot—Mr. Steely.

"And you thought I was crazy," said Mrs. Truffle seated on the other side of him. "I think you're the one having a nervous breakdown."

"Yeah!" whistled Bradley. "You can't quit on me now, you scaredy-cat."

Henry glanced up from his sketch with a pale, sweaty face. The flashing newspaper cameras made him flinch several times, swirling his eyes with a slideshow of memories. Starting with his third grade classroom, he was writing a letter to Santa, followed by his frantic tearing through the stocking. Stale Hershey's kisses peppered the air . . . a pair of unlucky dice tumbled to the carpet . . . but no Mr. Steely.

"I hate you Santa, you fat, lying, dirty bastard." Henry suddenly realized he wasn't lashing out in a flashback, but was declaring war on Santa right here in the courtroom.

"I guess that means you're ready for trial," said Nora, to the glee of Bradley and Mrs. Truffle.

Eight

Outside the courthouse, the crowd grew larger than the Macy's Parade on Thanksgiving. After all, it was no longer some poor slob dressed up as Santa they were waiting to see. Just weeks before Christmas, the real Saint Nick had blessed them with his appearance.

Still parked on the street was his sleigh. A pack of middle school kids climbed up on it, careful not to disturb anything, since they would now be hanging stockings once again. Some fifth graders pet his reindeer and fed them everything from apples to Baby Ruth bars. Even the strictest of traffic officers was willing to ignore the "Loading Only" sign that cast a shadow on Santa's unlicensed vehicle.

More news vans arrived, cutting through the crowd like angry bees. Reporters Patrick Carol and Carol Patrick stood their ground on the courthouse steps. Facing their TV camera, they shouted over the excitement:

"Carol, I don't think New Yorkers have been this happily surprised since the Mets won the pennant back in '69."

"You're right, Patrick. The arrival of Santa has turned the hardest of men into believers." She turned to a beefy crew of construction workers. "Hey guys. Why don't you tell us what you saw?"

"We was up on 'dat thirty story ledge," said the construction foreman, pointing up at a skyscraper under repair, "when Santa came rippin' by on his sled."

The workers nodded in their helmets. "We'd've saved 'em some milk 'n cookies had we known he was droppin' by." They held up their metal lunchboxes with stubbly faces showing regret.

Nine

Such testimony was still not enough for Trish Milton. Seated with Junior in front of the TV, she flipped through one station after another, only to see more confirming reports:

"Ho-ho-ho," said a weathered anchorman who suddenly looked ten years younger. "Guess who's coming to town?" A replay courtesy of Action-7 News showed Santa flying in on his sleigh.

"You'd better not pout; you'd better not cry," said Karen Burke on Channel-5.

A shirtless degenerate in a Santa's cap appeared on Public Access. "Whoa dudes, Santa Claus is like here in the Big Apple."

"With the shocking arrival of Saint Nick," reported a more serious-looking chap on the BBC.

After flipping through every channel, Trish finally stared at the screen in numb disbelief. Another countless replay showed Santa's appearance in the sky.

"What's the matter, Mom? I thought you believed in Santa?"

"I did, I do, it's just that. . ." She watched Henry exit the courthouse on TV. If Santa wasn't a big enough surprise, now she was watching her husband—soon to be ex-husband—becoming a media sensation.

Henry looked more handsome than ever as he coolly addressed the reporters: "You're the ones who thought this was some kind of cheap publicity stunt. But Santa Claus is real; and now I have to get to work to prove he did real harm to my client." Like a concerned father, he led his pudgy client away.

The boy's mother followed, along with some hot young vixen in a business suit.

Suspecting she was Henry's new girlfriend, Trish wanted to claw her out of the TV screen and shatter her on the floor of their apartment, the one she and Henry had struggled for years to pay the mortgage on.

"She's not nearly as pretty as you are, Mom."

Trish turned to her sweet little boy who was looking more like his father every day. "Thank you, honey." She knew he was telling the truth, even if she didn't believe it herself.

As Santa exited the courthouse on TV, she turned up the volume in hopes of drowning out the jealous thoughts in her head. "Let's see what Santa has to say."

Ten

"Ho-ho-ho!" were the first words out of Santa's chapped and burning lips. Next time he'd remember his Chapstick before flying over the windy Atlantic; but that didn't stop him from smiling and waving to his cheering crowd of supporters.

"Mr. Claus!" shouted Patrick Carol over the fanfare. "How are you prepared to fight this lawsuit?"

"You should really ask my lawyers," said Santa, unable to spot his little elves in the throng of reporters. Turning to Carol Patrick, he said, "My wife's a big fan of your show. She really appreciates your workout tips."

"Thank you, Santa. Did she try my butt burners?"

"Boy did she ever, and you should see 'er in 'er gym tights."

"In the meantime," said Patrick, slightly annoyed, "How will this trial affect your toy operations at the North Pole?"

"Well, I'm afraid I may not be bringing any presents this year."

Several children burst into tears, their wailing cries drifting like cold fog over the festivities.

"Don't cry, kids! Your parents can fill your stockings this year! They usually help me anyway!"

"But Santa!" a grimy little boy cried out. "The toy store doesn't take my mom's food stamps!"

Santa peered down on the boy with a disheartened smile. "Next year, kid. I promise."

Eleven

The airwaves delivered that message to televisions across the world. Whether in Chile, Japan, Russia, France, or Norway, the viewers didn't need to speak English to understand Santa's words. All they needed was the image of Santa hugging that grimy little boy who now sobbed into his beard.

Next year, Santa had promised. Next year, meaning thousands of children would be deprived of Christmas presents this year.

"This is all Dad's fault," said Junior, turning off the TV. "And I'm gonna go straighten 'em out." Grabbing his Yankees cap and jacket, he headed out the door before his mother could stop him.

"Stay off the subway!" she called after him. "And be home before dark!"

Twelve

Henry's office was a madhouse of visitors and ringing phones.

"You're gonna have to hire a secretary," said Nora, punching one line after the next to keep up with callers.

Swarmed by kids and their parents, Henry frantically jotted down their noisy complaints.

"Santa gave me this skateboard," said a skater punk with a cast on his arm. "The wheel came off and that's how I busted my wrist."

"What's your name, son?"

"They call me Max Wheeler, dude."

"My name's Shelly Sheepshank," said a bratty girl with a gaping smile. "Santa gave me this jawbreaker, and that's how I broke my teeth." She handed over the evidence, which Henry reluctantly took in his bare palm.

"Can we sue the tooth fairy, too?" asked her weasel-faced father, Mr. Sheepshank.

Before Henry could answer, a notoriously wealthy family pressed forward in stuffy attire that matched their expressions. From photos of socialite events in the newspaper, Henry instantly recognized them as the Whitfields: Mr. and Mrs. Whitfield with their prissy twin daughters, Blaire and Blaine, nicknamed the "B-B Twins" by some of the local tabloids for their elementary school pranks, which included firing a B-B gun loaded with raisins at their school mascot—some poor substitute teacher in a beaver costume.

According to Mr. Whitfield, "Santa knocked over a vase" in their Park Avenue home.

"Worth a hundred-thousand dollars," reported Mrs. Whitfield.

"And he didn't even give us the ruby earrings we asked for," whined Blaire.

"He gave us pearls," said Blaine in disgust.

"We have everything on tape." Mr. Whitfield shoved a surveillance video at Henry.

"Okay, I'll take a look at this soon as—"

Massive cleavage quickly distracted Henry from the tape. A pretty yet hardened woman spoke to him in a sultry voice: "Santa came into my bedroom and called me a ho. Three times, ho-ho-ho." Smiling at Henry, she closed her fur coat over her skimpy top. "Hi, Mr. Milton. I'm Rene Reno."

"Is that your real name?" said Henry, as if she might be a stripper or adult film star.

"Yes it is," said Rene Reno. "And just because men find me attractive doesn't give that dirty old man the right to come down my chimney and harass me. 1 want a million bucks. Unless he wants Mrs. Claus to know what went down that night."

"Can you be more specific?" said Henry a bit too eagerly.

"Henry!" shouted Nora in a girlfriend tone of voice. "Calls are coming in from across the country! Everyone in America wants you!"

Including you, thought Henry with a little wink.

"I was first!" Bradley shrilled from the couch. "I'm the reason they're calling! That's why all these people are here!"

"That's right, sweetie," said Mrs. Truffle, feeding her son a Ritz cracker. "And Mr. Milton owes you for it."

"I'm definitely grateful," said Henry. "But I can't ignore all these wonderful people who need my help."

That started another frenzy of kids and parents tearing at him from all directions. Trying to listen and take notes, Henry didn't recognize a voice that should've sounded familiar:

"I really need to talk to you!"

"What's your name, young man?"

"Henry Milton," the voice dryly responded.

Henry looked up in surprise to see his son. "Junior! Don't tell me! You're here to sue Santa!"

"NO DAD, I WANT YOU TO END THIS BULL—ONEY! NOW!"

The office turned silent, as if a lightning bolt had struck.

"We'll talk about this later, okay? Soon as I'm done here."

Nora punched her phone lines on hold with a forced smile. "Can I get you a Pepsi while you're waiting?"

"I'm not thirsty."

"Let's take a seat next to Bradley here." Henry led his son toward the couch. "You can have some of his crackers."

Bradley guarded the box with his fat body. "Stay away from me, loser. I don't care who your daddy is." The whistle rattled in his throat.

"Dad?" said Junior in dismay. "You'd rather spend your day with him than me?"

"Come on, Junior." Henry dragged his son inside a cubicle. "This is my career here."

Junior gazed at a fading Polaroid of his family at Coney Island. "I wish you were a janitor like Billy Binder's dad. He gets off at 2:30 every day and plays video games and all kinds 'a cool stuff."

"You don't really mean that. I'll get one-third of what all these people are asking."

"They're stealing from Santa."

"One-third Junior. Do you know what that means? You could be going to an Ivy League school. Driving a Beamer across campus. A future I could never dream of as a boy your age."

"I just want you to do what's right, Dad."

"That's why I became a lawyer, son. To balance the scales of injustice."

"Just 'cause Santa didn't bring you any toys."

"I wouldn't want anything from that ruthless tyrant."

"You must've done something pretty bad to be on his naughty list."

"I did not! I was a good boy! Worked hard in school! Cleaned my room! Brushed my teeth! Minded my—"

"I don't believe you. And neither did Santa." Junior fled the cubicle, leaving Henry alone in the time capsule of photos.

"Junior! Wait!" Henry chased after his son, but was quickly surrounded by his mob of new clients.

"He'll be okay," said Nora. With a pleased smile, she watched Junior leave the office.

Thirteen

The Christmas tree was left half-decorated in the Miltons' living room. With Henry not there to help this year, Trish and Junior had lost enthusiasm halfway through the Elvis Presley Christmas album.

"Merry Christmas Baby" had always been Henry's musical inspiration for hanging bobbles and tinsel. Trish would've preferred the Beach Boys singing "Little Saint Nick" or "The Man with all the Toys" but those songs were too corny for Henry, who hated anything to do with Santa. Come to think of it, Trish was surprised he'd ever participated in one of their few family traditions.

While Elvis may have been silenced, Henry's spirit lingered in the room, which Trish had turned into her artist's workshop. Some rearranging of furniture made space for what Henry used to call her hobby, though Trish didn't consider her sculptures a hobby at all, proven by the expensive price tags on them. For the holidays, she had carved out figurines of winter skaters, a Nutcracker soldier, and of course, Santa with his reindeer and elves, which were clearly in demand.

At the moment, Trish was carving a life-sized bust of an angel, by far her most ambitious project yet. Done with its serenely pretty face, Trish now sculpted the wings—feather after feather taking hour after hour. As she whittled away the time, she got lost in the dark crevices of her work, a meditative place where she sorted out the details of her failed marriage.

Unable to pinpoint where she and Henry had started to drift apart, she thought back to where it all began. In a college cafeteria line, Henry had tried bumping her out of the way for that last slice of chocolate cake. An ensuing argument somehow led to a date, but only after Trish had eaten the last nibble of frosting. Truthfully, she didn't even care much for desserts, but she did enjoy the sweet taste of victory over a cocky law student.

A week later, their first real dinner date was barely a step above the cafeteria. In a cheap Italian restaurant filled with students, Trish bit into a piece of crunchy garlic bread that popped the veneer off her front tooth. At best, she looked like an attractive parolee who'd busted her way outta the joint. At worst, a female boxer after losing a brutal match.

Right then, most guys would've made an excuse to call it an early night. *Got a final exam, gotta get home and study, blah-blah-blah.* But not Henry. In fact, he laughed so hard he spilled their pitcher of root beer into his lap, making it appear he'd wet his pants.

On their walk home that night, they looked like a drunken homeless couple. Instead of feeling self-conscious about her looks, Trish never felt more beautiful, simply by the way Henry was looking at her. The fact she was a couple of inches taller didn't seem to bother him either. Perhaps he was always too busy looking ahead to even notice he was on the short side. Before they even made it to bed on date nine, (though Henry would still argue "lucky" number seven) he was talking marriage, kids, and future law practice.

Now, as Trish tried carving an angel to life, she could barely remember what they'd even talked about on that very first date. Classes perhaps. She was an art major; he was in law school. They agreed it was an unlikely match, which only made things all the more exciting. Add a full moon in springtime and they were waltzing into a relationship. But then again, wasn't that how most relationships started? Dinner, moonlight, laughter. Minus the broken tooth and wet pants, that is.

An opening door jarred Trish from her thoughts.

Junior entered the apartment with a discouraged look. "Now I'm beginning to understand why you wanted a divorce."

"What's the matter, sweetie?"

"If I had to have a lawyer for a father, I wish it would've been one of Santa's elves." Junior shuffled off to his room and closed the door behind him.

"I may find short men cute. But really."

Fourteen

It was well after dark before the last client finally left Henry's office, the elderly Mrs. Fudderbug who swore Santa had kidnapped her precious cat Bootsie.

Even Henry had a hard time accepting this case. He'd sent Mrs. Fudderbug away needing some proof of Bootsie's abduction. If confirmed, poor Bootsie would need ski boots to survive a winter in the North Pole.

"I never knew Santa had so many enemies," said Nora, pouring through a blizzard of faxes that had come in from across the nation. "And this is before we ran out of paper."

Henry riffled through them until he found what he was looking for. "Here we go. A listing of Santa's assets."

Nora read over his shoulder in amazement. "His North Pole Operations is worth ten *billion* dollars."

"More than all the major toy factories combined."

"With all these new clients, think of the settlement."

Henry eagerly nodded. "First things first, though. I'd better get ready for ol' whistling Bradley tomorrow." Pouring fresh coffee, he opened Bradley's file.

"Henry? You realize this is gonna be the Trial of the Century."

Henry looked up from the file. "I just wish Junior could understand. That someday he'll be thanking me for all of this."

"You do have someone who appreciates you." Nora rubbed his shoulders with a seductive touch.

Henry smiled and shut his eyes with a soft groan.

"Looks like you could use a little stress release," she whispered with hot breath in his ear. Turning to close the blinds, she let her hair down before turning back to Henry with a button open on her blouse.

Like a scene from gritty film noir, Henry pulled her into his lap for a kiss. The kiss got steamier than the coffee he pushed aside with Bradley's file. After a very long day, work would have to wait for pleasure.

It was gonna be a sleepless night for the most wanted lawyer in America.

Fifteen

Next morning, Henry sat with Nora in the plaintiff's row of a crowded courtroom. With trial scheduled to begin in just a few minutes, Henry anxiously checked his watch. "Where the heck are my clients?"

"I dunno, but take a look at those two—"

In the media section were Patrick Carol and Carol Patrick. Thanks to Judge Thorne, no TV cameras would be allowed inside, but that didn't stop the reporting duo from a last minute grooming.

"How's my hair look?"

"Same as always. Anything on my teeth?" Carol smiled to reveal a stringy piece of spinach.

Henry chuckled. "I hope she does her live broadcast like that."

"Me too," said Nora. "Look how they're fawning over Santa."

The two reporters playfully chatted with Santa and his elf lawyers in the defense row.

"It's about time," said Henry, as his motley crew of clients finally lumbered in. Sporting a purple Mohawk, Max Wheeler saluted Henry with his arm cast before taking a seat next to Shelly Sheepshank. Shelly smiled to reveal her broken teeth from the jawbreaker. Mr. Sheepshank plopped down beside her in a cheap wrinkled suit and overpowering cologne. In complete contrast were Mr. and Mrs. Whitfield in posh business attire. Their B-B Twins, Blaire & Blaine, looked like Sunday school girls in their matching dresses and hair bows; while Rene Reno appeared in a devilish red skirt and spiked heels. To Mr. Sheepshank's dismay, she squeezed into a seat next to Bradley Truffle. Bradley, too young to appreciate her skimpy attire, unwrapped candies with help from his doting mother.

"Glad to see you're all here," said Henry with a friendly wave down the row.

His clients responded with a noisy chorus of complaints, things they had forgotten to mention in his office the day before.

"Order in the court!" Judge Thorne's hammering gavel brought instant silence. "All rise!"

Henry sprung to his feet. "Your Honor! I motion for a class action!"

"Class action?" Judge Thorne peered over his bifocals at Henry's inflated row.

"Yes, your Honor. Only a handful of my clients are present today, but as you can see, my office has received thousands of complaints against Mr. Claus." Henry gestured to a line of boxes beneath his bench, each of them overstuffed with files.

Judge Thorne sternly gazed over them. "Before I will consider a motion of this magnitude, I must first hear from your clients in attendance. If you can demonstrate that the defendant, Mr. Claus, was in fact negligent, I will schedule a hearing for a class action settlement."

"I can do better than that." Henry watched Santa and his elf lawyers squirm in the defense row. "I'm going to prove to the court, and the world, that Santa Claus is a menace to society."

The audience gasped in horror.

"How can you say that?" blurted Santa, marching into the aisle. "I bring toys to children! You—" His elf lawyers quickly pulled him back.

"Yeah, well you forgot about one of those kids, Santa."

Sixteen

Bradley Truffle was first to take the stand, his face smudged with chocolate despite his mother's efforts to wipe it off. He sourly watched Henry approach with a magic elf whistle.

"Does this look like the whistle that is now lodged between your lingual tonsil and vocal chord?" Henry turned to an anatomical chart of the human throat, with a whistle stuck in it.

"Yes," Bradley twittered like a sick bird.

Henry handed over the shiny instrument. "Could you please read the warning on it?"

Bradley stared blankly at it. "How can I? There isn't one."

"Then how could you possibly know the dangers involved?"

"I didn't!"

"Of course not," said Henry with a somber smile at his client. "I know this is difficult, Bradley. But could you please tell the court how your life has changed since swallowing the magic elf whistle?"

"Well, I have to go around talking like this."

The audience laughed at his shrilling voice.

"And everyone keeps laughing at me!" Choking back tears, Bradley looked to his mother for help.

The courtroom turned shamefully quiet.

Henry spoke in a nurturing tone: "Do the kids at school make fun of you?"

"Yeah. They call me names, like the Human Teakettle or Whistling Pete."

"But your name is Bradley."

"I don't know who I am anymore."

"Before this tragic accident, what was your dream in life?"

"To become a famous Broadway singer. I had a part lined up in *Peter Pan*."

Mrs. Truffle leapt to her feet in the plaintiff's row. "My son could've been the next Michael Bolton!"

The audience groaned in protest.

"I think you mean Frank Sinatra," said Henry. "Right Pete? I mean Bradley!"

"It doesn't matter now," sobbed Bradley. "My life is ruined. I'm nobody."

"I'm very sorry, young man." Henry peered over the audience of saddened faces. Even Judge Thorne and Santa Claus showed pity in their expressions.

"I'm finished with my client, your Honor."

Seventeen

Junior was the only one in his third grade classroom not wearing a T-shirt pronouncing: I SUPP♥RT SANTA. Not that he didn't share their feelings. He was simply afraid of his father's reaction if he happened to be caught in it. As son of the lawyer suing Santa, Junior was not safe from reporters taking his photo. During morning recess, paparazzi had been escorted off the playground by Mrs. Rizzo, his feisty old teacher now writing math problems on the board.

Mrs. Rizzo turned to the class to reveal she too was a Santa Supporter, proven by the slogan on her drooping chest. "Okay, you little Einsteins. Let's see how far you've come."

Deana Grigsby, the cutest girl in class, quickly raised her hand. "Mrs. Rizzo? Are we gonna write letters to Santa this year?"

Archie Browning, the class bully who'd once made Junior eat a spider, turned to Deana with a disgusted look. "Haven't you been watchin' the news? Thanks to somebody's dad, there ain't gonna be no Santa this year."

Everyone turned to stare at Junior, who quickly ducked behind the shield of an open history book. "I-I-I support Santa," he stammered from his desk.

"Let's not blame Junior for what his father does," advised Mrs. Rizzo.

"But his dad is a scumbag," said the smelly Billy Binder, whose SANTA T-shirt hadn't been washed after several days of wear.

"Nobody makes fun of you because your father scrubs toilets for a living," said Mrs. Rizzo.

"I do," said Archie Browning, which got a rise from the class.

"Just like we don't make fun of your dad for being in prison," said Mrs. Rizzo.

"He's up for parole next month," said Archie, glaring back at Junior. "And when he gets outta the joint, I'm gonna have my dad beat up your dad!"

"Nobody's going to beat anyone up," said Mrs. Rizzo unconvincingly.

"Please, you guys!" Junior pleaded. "I never wanted this to happen."

"I bet you'll have all the toys in the world once your dad gets done with Santa," said Archie.

"Yeah," the class chimed in.

"Back to work, everyone," said Mrs. Rizzo.

The angry students finally turned their attention to their math problems.

Overwhelmed by their attack, Junior dismally gazed into his history book. A photo of a ragged GI was captioned with the infamous quote: "War is hell."

For Junior, that was third grade.

Eighteen

From having read his interview in the paper, Henry knew the following about his opposing lead counsel: Educated at Harvard Law School, Mr. Elfsquire was often mistaken for a dwarf or midget by his peers and professors, who couldn't possibly believe in an elf. As the smallest man on campus, he'd worked hard to prove that size doesn't define ability.

After graduating number one in his class, Mr. Elfsquire was recruited by the top law firms in Boston and New York. Though tempted by their tall offers, the little elf returned to the North Pole, where he trained and assembled the legal team present today. For years, Mr. Elfsquire had foreseen the inevitable lawsuit against Santa, and now he was here, in New York City, cross examining Bradley on the stand.

"Could you please show the court how you were using the instrument?"

Bradley hesitated before playing a little tune on the magic elf whistle.

"Very nice," said Mr. Elfsquire. "I bet you can produce some amazing sounds when you use your teeth."

"I don't play with my teeth," trilled Bradley, his voice wavering uncertainly like a beginning flutist playing a scale.

"Oh? Really? Then perhaps you can explain what these little marks are from?" Mr. Elfsquire produced a blown-up copy of the X-ray, which clearly revealed tiny bite marks on the whistle stuck in Bradley's throat.

"I dunno." Bradley squeamishly unwrapped a piece of candy.

"Do those look like bite marks to you?"

"I dunno."

"You wouldn't happen to be a nervous eater, would you?"

"No." Bradley plopped the candy in his mouth and chewed with hard crunches.

The audience perked up in their seats.

Judge Thorne leaned forward and turned up his hearing aid.

"I told him not to eat on the stand," whispered Henry to Nora in the plaintiff's row.

"You should've checked his pockets."

"He's just a growing boy!" Mrs. Truffle announced to the courtroom.

"Sit down, Mrs. Truffle!" ordered Judge Thorne.

"But your mother is correct," said Mr. Elfsquire to Bradley. "And might you recall if you were hungry at the time you swallowed the whistle?"

Bradley's stomach growled. "If I was, it's all my mom's fault. Takes her forever to make me a stupid sandwich."

"Were you waiting for lunch while playing the whistle?"

Bradley anxiously unwrapped another piece of candy. "Maybe, I dunno."

"Please answer the question," said Judge Thorne impatiently.

"Yeah, but so what?" Bradley stuffed the candy in his mouth and choked on it.

"I think you just answered your own question," said Mr. Elfsquire. "And mine too."

As Bradley gagged on the candy with widening eyes, an anxious murmur swept over the courtroom.

"Don't do this to me kid," muttered Henry.

"Somebody help my baby!" cried Mrs. Truffle.

Mr. Elfsquire gave a jolting slap to Bradley's back. The candy plopped out of his mouth with a whistling cough.

"That's all for now, your Honor." Mr. Elfsquire winked at Henry on the way back to his seat.

Nineteen

The final bell sounded like a war siren at Public School No. 27 in the Bronx. Exactly twenty-seven years after Henry wrote his last letter to Santa, his son followed his traceless footsteps across the playground.

Of course, Junior was oblivious to such family history, since his father never disclosed his childhood. Had Junior been looking up, as his father would learn to do, he might have seen a message in those blackened rain clouds: Watch out, Buster, because perched on the bars above were Archie Browning and his gang of thugs.

They dropped down on Junior like a sudden avalanche. A flash of light in his skull preceded a smothering darkness. The taste of dirt filled his mouth. A storm of fists swept over his body. Through ringing ears, he heard Archie say: "At least my dad robs banks, not Kris Kringle," followed by the cheers of students gathered to watch his defeat.

Somewhere in the bottom of that pile, Junior managed to land an elbow to someone's nose. According to his father, he should never accept defeat lying down.

Thanks, Dad, but where are you now?

Twenty

Henry was fighting his own battle in the courtroom. After that Harvard-trained midget—dwarf—elf—had shown him up, he'd decided to go straight at the enemy by calling Mr. Santa Claus, defendant, to the stand.

"Mr. Claus. Do you recall putting a magic elf whistle in my client's stocking last Christmas Eve?"

"Vaguely. I gave out thousands of those things."

"But your records show you did?"

"Yes, thanks to my elves' computers."

The audience thought that was funny. Henry annoyingly waited for their laughter to simmer down. "Are you aware that twelve children were sent to the hospital last year for choking on your magic elf whistles?"

Santa squirmed in his seat. "No, actually I wasn't."

"Are your toys even tested to meet federal safety guidelines?"

Santa's forehead beaded with sweat; he loosened his furry red coat in the stuffy courtroom. "This is the only country that has such a thing."

"Are you implying that such guidelines are ridiculous?"

"A little perhaps."

A startled gasp arose from the audience.

"So does that explain why no warning comes on the toy?"

"The toys are designed to be played with, not eaten like gummy bears."

"Do you realize that kids often put things in their mouths?"

"Guess I'm a kid at heart," whispered Rene Reno, seductively licking one of Bradley's lollypops.

"It's a whistle!" exclaimed Santa. "How else can it work?"

"And knowing this," said Henry, "Why didn't you design it so it couldn't be swallowed?"

"Well, I never thought—"

"That your toys were capable of harming innocent children?"

"I simply give them what they ask for!"

"So if Johnny's a good boy and wants a hand grenade?"

"Objection!" said Mr. Elfsquire.

"Withdrawn. I'm done with this witness for today, your Honor."

Judge Thorne tapped his gavel. "Court adjourned. We'll resume at oh-nine-hundred tomorrow."

A worried hum passed over the audience.

Henry noticed many of those ridiculous T-shirts: I SUPP♥RT SANTA. "He's gonna need it," he told Nora, as they led their circus of clients out of the courtroom.

Twenty-One

Junior was not allowed to ride the subway train unless coming home from school with a group of classmates. According to his mother, there was safety in numbers. What she'd failed to mention were those numbers turning against you. Like bad odds in Vegas, his classmates stacked against him twenty-to-one, leaving him to stand by himself at the opposite end of the subway car.

Junior's head and body throbbed from the playground fight. Afraid to look at his reflection in the window, his curiosity finally made him inventory the damage: Swollen black eye. Cracked and bent glasses. Fat lip. Scratches and bruises over face and body. Torn Yankees jacket. NY cap missing, probably somewhere on the playground, where he could've been beaten a lot worse. With so many punks on top of him, they'd actually blocked each other's punches.

Now Junior was enduring the nosy stares from other passengers, except his classmates who kept their backs to him. Hopefully nobody would recognize him as Henry Milton, Junior. If so, he might be facing another assault before the next stop. Perhaps he should take karate, or at least buy faster running shoes.

As the train rumbled ahead, he noticed several riders ducked behind a popular tabloid. On the cover was the headline: SATAN VS. SANTA? A caricature portrayed his father as a horned devil, sticking his pitchfork up the chimney at Santa's tush.

Junior overheard two businessmen talking over their papers:

"And I thought the lawyer who settled my divorce was a scumbag."

"Just last week, nobody knew who this guy was. Now he's the most famous lawyer in the world."

"Maybe he made a deal with the devil."

"Or maybe this Henry Milton really is the devil."

The businessmen laughed and turned their pages.

"That's Henry Milton, Senior," Junior corrected them.

The men looked inquisitively over their papers.

Before they could guess he was truly the son of Satan, the train screeched to a halt and Junior exited five stops short of his usual departure. He could walk the rest of the way by himself, since his classmates wouldn't be waiting for him anyway.

Twenty-Two

The New York City Police Department wasn't sure what to do about the growing crowd outside the courthouse. Not since the Sixties had there been so many chanting and waving signs: "Support Santa!" At least they were upholding tradition instead of protesting like a bunch of damn hippies. That is why several officers piled out of an armored truck without shields or tear gas.

Nothing in the Big Apple's history could compete with this fanfare. Not the Beatles playing Shea Stadium. Or Reggie Jackson's five home runs in the World Series. Or the Miracle Mets. Thanks to Saint Nick, their fans down in Queens were beginning to believe in miracles once again.

From every borough they came to cheer Santa. Thousands more arrived from across the nation and world, hoping to confirm what they'd seen on TV. A group from the Midwest proved this point with matching sweatshirts: DEAR SANTA: COME TO MISSOURI AND WE'LL BELIEVE.

A sudden booing erupted from the crowd as Henry exited the courthouse. Reporters Patrick Carol and Carol Patrick chased after him with their microphones. "Mr. Milton! Do you feel you've jumped to an early advantage after day one of trial?"

Henry smiled at the media duo. "Well, Patrick. That's not for me to say. But if you thought today was a surprise, just wait until tomorrow."

"Any tricks up your sleeve?" asked Carol.

An egg splattered on Henry's overcoat. He glared into the crowd in hopes of spotting the heckler who'd thrown it. "I'll save the dirty tricks for Santa and his fans. I'm gonna beat 'em with the cold, hard facts."

Henry bustled past the jeering crowd, many shouting names that were unfit for television. Nora and his clients scurried after him, ducking beneath umbrellas as a hailstorm of eggs came down.

Twenty-Three

Trish was watching Henry on TV, unsure whether to pity him or join the booing crowd when Junior walked in the door, looking far worse than someone attacked by eggs.

"Oh my God! What happened?"

Junior peered at her through his swollen black eye and broken glasses. "Can I change my name? Move to a country that doesn't celebrate Christmas?"

"Who did this to you? I'm gonna call their parents. The school principal!"

"How 'bout Japan? You can call me Yo, short for Yoshi."

"You're thinking of that sushi bar, and they actually go crazy over Christmas in Japan."

"They do? How 'bout Saudi Arabia?"

"Oh, sweetie." Trish swept her darling little boy into her arms. "We need to get some ice on this. Clean up these cuts. Why would anyone do this to my baby?"

Junior watched his father escaping the jeering crowd on TV. "Gee, I wonder."

Trish turned to see Henry getting into a cab with that little tramp who was supposedly his publicity manager.

"Well, I hope your father is proud of himself."

Twenty-Four

Seated in the back of the cab with Nora, Henry was feeling very proud of himself. "Fourth and Madison," he yelled out to the driver.

"You're taking us to Adele's?" Pleasantly surprised, Nora was referring to an upscale French restaurant that had recently opened.

"A little celebration for our first-round victory."

They kissed, hugged, and kissed some more.

Henry could almost taste his first glass of champagne when his cell phone rang. Seeing Trish's name as the caller, he nervously apologized to Nora: "She only calls when it's an emergency."

Before he could say the "lo" in "Hello," he had two angry women to contend with. Nora was glaring at him like a tiger ready to pounce, while Trish screamed in his ear that he was the worst father in the world, proven by their son getting beaten up at . . . Static cut into the line as they whizzed beneath an overhang.

"He what?" Henry said in alarm. "Is he okay? No stitches or anything?"

"He's gonna be fine," blared Trish's voice in his ear. "But what he really needs is some emotional support."

"Want me to go beat up those little punks?" Henry considered the new breed of hoodlums in the Bronx. "How big are they?"

"No, I don't want you to beat up a bunch of eight-year-olds! I want you to talk to Junior."

"Okay, I'll be right over. Soon as I pick up a little surprise for 'em."

"The only surprise he needs right now is for his father to show up early."

"Tell 'em I'm on my way." Henry hung up and gave Nora a weary smile. "It's Junior. Some kids at school beat 'em up."

"Yeah, I kinda got that. What a shame." She stared out the window in disappointment.

Henry started to apologize, but decided against it. They would ride in silence until they got to their new destination. "Driver. Take us to that new toy store on Amsterdam and eighty-second."

Twenty-Five

Planet Toys was truly like entering another planet, especially for Henry, who hadn't been in a toy store since the third grade, the year he gave up on being a kid.

He was amazed by the high-tech action figures of today, powered by remote controls instead of windups. They'd sure come a long way since Mr. Steely, which he surprisingly didn't see on the shelves. A strange feeling came over him, like a guy half hoping to run into his ex-girlfriend, but relieved not to be reminded of what he'd lost.

As he whisked Nora through the store, he noticed several kids and their parents giving him strange looks. "They're onto me," he said, ducking into the costume aisle, where he donned zany glasses, fake mustache, and tweed cap.

Nora watched him in embarrassment. "That's only going to draw more attention."

Henry admired himself on the security monitor. "I look like a mad professor."

"Unfortunately, I'd have to agree."

"Oh well. People don't throw things at zany intellects." 'Professor' Milton proceeded down the next aisle in his egg-stained coat. An arsenal of toys quickly made him forget he was shopping for Junior.

"Oh cool! Look at this!" Henry grabbed a purple air rifle that shot Styrofoam balls. Charging down the aisle, he fired at teddy bears that dropped off the shelf. "Pow! Pow! Pow!"

"Really, Henry. Let's just pick something out and—"

"Wow! It's been forever since I've been in a toy store. Check this out!" Henry snatched a mini-basketball and took aim on a digital hoop that beeped and flashed his point total.

"Henry, we've got a very tight schedule."

"Come on, Nora, take a shot!" Henry tossed the ball at her.

Nora stepped aside, letting it roll down the aisle.

"It's not gonna hurt you!" Henry chased it down and dribbled back to the hoop. Halfway there, he was intercepted by a group of kids eager to play.

"You got no game," said one boy in a tough Brooklyn accent.

"Oh yeah, let's see if you can stop me." Henry tried dribbling through them, but their mauling defense ripped his hat, mustache and glasses off. "Time out! That's a foul!" Henry fumbled to straighten his costume when the toughies pointed him out.

"Hey! You're that lawyer guy on TV!"

"That butthead suin' Santa."

"Give it up, loser."

The boys mugged Henry of the basketball.

"Technical foul!" he called, breaking loose from the little hooligans.

Nora awaited him a safe distance away. "Are you finally ready?"

"Yeah. Let's go!" Henry grabbed a box containing the digital hoop and escaped toward the register.

"Junior's gonna love this."

Twenty-Six

Henry stepped out of Planet Toys and returned to Earth. New York City to be precise, with its dazzling shop windows lit for Christmas, its sidewalks packed with holiday shoppers. Out of costume, Henry ducked behind the box to conceal his face.

Nora followed him out with a deep inhale of cold night air. "I couldn't breathe in that place. All those bratty kids."

"Not all kids are brats," Henry said defensively.

"Oh, no, I didn't say they were."

"Junior's a good boy. He was just a little upset that day he came into my office."

"Just a little? I'd hate to see him really angry."

"He doesn't normally have outbursts like that."

"Good to know. I don't think he liked me very much."

"He's going through a tough time. Besides, I'm not looking for someone to be his stepmother. He already has a mom, a super terrific mom."

"Yeah," said Nora, inflecting both relief and jealousy.

They walked in silence, trying to find something to turn the conversation. Passing a jewelry store window, Nora discovered it. "Oh, look!" She pulled Henry over to admire a sparkling diamond necklace on display.

"Very nice," said Henry, feeling her breast against his arm.

"You could put that on my Christmas list," she suggested with a smile.

Henry nodded with troubled thoughts. Before he married Trish, he'd promised her a diamond wedding ring, but she'd insisted on investing in their future.

"What's the matter?"

"Nothing. I'd better get home before Junior thinks I stood 'em up."

"Home? You don't live there anymore."

Henry nodded and broke away from her clutching embrace.

Twenty-Seven

At his former residence, Henry stumbled through the door with the hefty box.

"You can't just buy him off," said Trish, helping him inside.

"I'm bringing him a present, something my old man never would've done."

"Just because you had a tough childhood doesn't mean Junior should be coming home with black eyes."

"I'll have a man-to-man with 'em."

"How 'bout a man-to-boy? Or father-to-son?"

Half-listening, Henry was paying more attention to the changes in the living room. "Looks like an art studio in here."

"It is. Just wish I had higher ceilings."

Glad to see I made space for you, Henry felt like saying.

"Don't look so disappointed, Henry. You were long gone before you ever moved out."

Henry silently nodded. The bust of a winged female mysteriously held his gaze. "Nice fairy."

"It's an angel, and it's not quite finished."

"Where's the halo?"

"Not all angels have halos."

"Then how can you tell the difference?"

"Angels rescue people. Fairies are just fairies, I guess."

"The Fairy Godmother helped rescue Cinderella."

"Okay, Henry. She's a fairy. Let's not waste our time arg—"

"She's beautiful, whatever she is."

"Well, coming from you, that's quite a compliment."

"Yeah. Remember how bored I used to get at those museums?"

"Oh, I remember. You were worse than taking a child."

Henry chuckled. "You're the one who threw a tantrum. Just for handing out a few of my cards."

"You were trying to hustle clients at a Picasso exhibit."

"He used hazardous materials. People were breathing that stuff in."

"It's artwork, Henry, and you can't sue a dead guy."

Henry opened his mouth with no response.

"I believe Junior's in his room," said Trish with a smile.

"Okay, thanks." Henry squeezed past her with the box, surprised to see strands of silver in his former lover's hair, her face marked by wrinkles like the grooves in her sculptures. Unchanging were her eyes, eternally sparked with girlish mischief. Caught in her bright green stare, Henry glimpsed a reflection of their past. Seated at a college diner were two poor students with a pitcher of root beer and a nine course entrée of dreams.

Twenty-Eight

The walls of Junior's room were a shrine to New York City sports teams. The Yankees, Jets, Knicks and Rangers appeared on pennants, posters, and calendars. Lining his shelves were model cars, a few stuffed bears that were starting to embarrass him, and a platoon of GI Joes and action figures.

Junior did not feel like playing with any of them. In bed he was resting after his mom had cleaned up his cuts, numbed his face with a bag of frozen peas (they were out of ice), and given him two aspirin that were supposed to make his head stop throbbing.

A frantic knocking on the door only made it worse. Before he could say "Come in," his father barged in with a box from Planet Toys.

"You awake, buddy? I got a surprise for ya!"

"Hey Dad," Junior said with little enthusiasm.

His father came over to examine his black eye and swollen lip. "Wow. You look like a pro hockey player. Soon you'll be playing with the big boys."

The NY Rangers toughly posed in their team photo.

"I wasn't 'playing' anything. I got my butt kicked on the schoolyard, all thanks to you."

His father took a seat on the edge of the bed. "This is a tough lesson that I'm sorry you have to learn so young."

"What? That people are gonna hate me for something I didn't do?"

"No. That people are always jealous of those with more."

"These guys on the subway were calling you the devil. It's in all the papers."

"And the bozos reading that trash would trade with me in a second."

"The kids at school say I'm gonna have all the toys in the world."

"That's my point, Junior. They want the toys for themselves. 'Cause their fathers don't bring home cool things like this—" His father tore open the box from Planet Toys.

Junior tried pretending he wasn't interested in what was inside.

"Come on, buddy. You gonna help me with this?"

Junior watched his father struggle with the packaging. Slowly he crawled out of bed for a better look. "What is this thing?"

"A mini-basketball hoop. To go right here in your room."

Junior perked up at the digital backboard. "Does it keep score?"

"Just wait and see," said his father with a smile. Wrestling with Styrofoam, he finally freed the contraption from its cardboard restraints.

Junior had never seen his father so excited. Not even when he settled a case against Durango Chili for a client who'd discovered a rat's tail in his canned dinner. (Durango argued it was a mouse, a much cuter rodent, and who could blame it for wanting a taste of the finest chili made in Texas?)

Rat or mouse, all that mattered now was his father mounting the backboard to the door with the "Easy to install" brackets, as the instruction manual promised.

Junior quickly unraveled the cord and plugged it in. The backboard lit up with red zeros for Player 1 and Player 2. A shot clock was set at 60, with a reset button available.

"You take the first shot," said his father, tossing him the mini-basketball.

Junior was all smiles as he launched a twelve-footer across the room.

Without realizing it, his head had stopped hurting.

Twenty-Nine

Inspired by Henry's response to her work, Trish was carving the final feathers of her angel's wings.

It was strange having him back in the house. For months, she hadn't seen him up close, except on television, which didn't reveal his sprouting gray hairs or growing creases around his eyes. Perhaps that hot little publicity manager was also his make-up artist.

Oh well. Trish was relieved to know he was aging on pace with her. Besides having two inches on Henry, she also had two years. Not that it mattered anymore, she quickly reminded herself.

From Junior's room came sounds of laughter and playful shouting. Whatever toy Henry brought made a wild beeping sound. Normally that might have annoyed her while she worked, like the neighbor's car alarm or Mrs. O'Neil's yapping poodle upstairs. But tonight, she only felt safe and peaceful in her apartment called home.

Thirty

It was Junior's turn to rebound. Through his swollen black eye, he watched his dad firing off shots from behind the desk chair/free throw line. As the digital clock ticked down, Senior had twenty seconds to match Junior's score of twenty-four.

"They didn't have cool stuff like this when I was a kid," said Henry, banking an off-balance shot off the ceiling. "Yes!"

Junior snagged the ball from the net and zinged it back. "What did you have for toys, Dad?"

Henry held the ball with faraway thoughts. "Well—all I really wanted was a Mr. Steely."

"What's that?"

"It was this cool robot toy. It could march upstairs, swim in the bathtub, and even speak in a commando voice."

"But you never got one?"

"Doesn't matter now," said Henry with a deflated grin. "I'm too old to be playing with toys." The buzzer sounded before he could launch his final shot. Junior had won by a dozen points.

"You're never too old to play, Dad. Just ask the Starman." Junior was referring to 'Starman' Starkowski, the 42-year-old Yankees pitcher on his wall.

"That's his job, son. I'm getting paid to be a lawyer."

"Maybe you should try something else?"

"If I could throw ninety-miles-an-hour, I wouldn't have to grow up either."

"Starman doesn't throw hard; he's a knuckleball pitcher."

"Oh yeah. Wasn't he suspended last year for throwing a spitter?"

"His arm was tired and hurting, and it was cold out."

"That's still cheating, and he let down all those kids who believed in 'em."

"I'm sorry you didn't get your Mr. Steely, Dad."

Thirty-One

The Pearly Gate Motel was a crumbling hellhole in the Bronx. Parked on the rooftop was Santa's sleigh. The line of reindeer was tended by a stable elf, one of the few non-lawyers to make the trip to New York.

The rest of the elves were inside a stuffy workout room on the fourth floor. In matching Polo sweats, they hoisted tiny dumbbells and took turns on battered machines.

Mr. Elfsquire tried showing off on a seated chin-up station. Pulling the bar down to his chest, he moved a huge stack of plates up the cable. In a swing of momentum, the bar shot upwards and so did Mr. Elfsquire. Suspended in midair, he desperately held on with his little feet dangling beneath him. "Someone get me down from here!"

A chorus of high-pitched laughter filled the room. Doubled over in hysteria, a rookie elf lawyer dropped a dumbbell on his size three Nike. "Objection!" he shouted, hopping around in agony.

In just as much pain was Santa on a rusty exercise bike. Wheezing for oxygen, he struggled to keep the pedals turning.

An elf trainer with biceps too big for his body monitored his activity. "Your blood pressure's going up with each day of trial."

"Maybe I'm getting closer to retirement than I thought."

"Who's going to take your place, sir?"

"They don't need me anymore. That's what this trial is really about."

A chubby elf lawyer approached with a tin of cookies. "Sir, a pack of Cub Scouts brought these for you. They're downstairs, waiting to have their picture taken."

"Ho-ho-ho! Glad to see there's still some good kids out there." Santa reached for a cookie, which his elf trainer snatched away.

"Time to start cutting back."

"It's only one cookie." Santa pedaled the bike with a sour frown.

"No pouting, Santa."

The elves burst into laughter, laughter so hard they fogged the mirrors. As if by magic, their reflections vanished from the misty glass.

Thirty-Two

The elf lawyers weren't laughing the next morning of trial. Nor was Santa's trainer, as Santa's blood pressure was most certainly rising. For the second day in a row, Henry had called him to the witness stand.

"Mr. Claus. On the night of December twenty-fourth of last year, do you recall entering the estate at Two-One-Three Park Avenue?"

"Beautiful neighborhood," said Santa. "The van Horn's left me pastries and espresso last year."

"How nice. But I really want to know about the Whitfields' home."

In the plaintiff's row, the uppity Whitfields straightened in their seats. The B-B Twins wore matching white dresses to appear as little angels. That was Nora's idea, seated beside them in black.

"Hmm," said Santa. "I really don't remember this family."

"You're not getting senile, are you?" said Henry.

"Objection!" shouted Mr. Elfsquire from the defense row.

"Sustained," said Judge Thorne, peering over his bifocals at the elf lawyer. "But I'd appreciate the courtesy of standing in my courtroom, counselor."

"I am standing, your Honor."

The courtroom erupted with laughter.

Even Santa joined in with a bellowing "Ho-ho-ho."

"Withdrawn," said Henry with a slight smirk. Approaching the courtroom TV, he inserted the surveillance video. "Perhaps this will help Santa's memory."

On TV, Santa came stumbling out of the fireplace with a half-empty bottle of whiskey.

The audience gasped in horror.

The Whitfields smugly watched the footage of their home: Santa teetered past their family portraits, tripping over a vase that toppled and shattered.

"That vase was from the Persian Empire," said Henry. "Its value was estimated at one-hundred-thousand dollars."

Judge Thorne painfully nodded at the TV. Santa was now raiding drawers of cash and jewelry that he stuffed in his red suit.

"That's not me!" pleaded Santa from the stand.

Caught on tape, he staggered toward a flower pot and unzipped his pants. Back turned to viewer, he took a long, splattering piss.

"Ewwww," the audience groaned in disgust.

Mrs. Truffle covered Bradley's eyes from such disgrace.

"Did Santa pee in my stocking?" he whistled.

"I'll be sure to wash it, darling."

"Not a bad idea," said Henry, finally freezing the video to face Santa in person. "Now do you remember, Mr. Claus?"

"I remember no such thing!"

"How much *were* you drinking that night?"

"I might've put a dab or two of whiskey in my eggnog, but only to keep me warm in that sleigh!"

"Looks like you had more than a dab, Mr. Claus." Henry resumed the video, which exposed Santa guzzling down the rest of the whiskey.

"That's an imposter! Another wannabe putting on the red suit and beard." Santa squinted at his alleged doppelganger on TV.

"Are you having trouble seeing the screen, Mr. Claus?"

"Must've forgotten my glasses." Santa patted his pockets in frustration.

"Perhaps you left them in the Whitfields' fireplace."

As Santa escaped up the chimney on TV, his glasses dropped out of his suit and landed in a rising plume of ash.

To the dread of the audience, Henry produced them from a handkerchief and blew the remaining dust off. "Here you go, Mr. Claus. Perhaps these will help you take a better look at yourself."

Santa bewilderedly put them on for a better view of the TV. "That guy has a bigger belly than me. And he needs to trim his beard. And shine those boots."

Henry turned to see the audience frowning; they clearly didn't see any difference between the two Santas. "Your Honor. In light of this evidence, I'm requesting on behalf of the people that Santa be charged on felony counts of breaking and entering, grand larceny, malicious mischief, and misusing public trust."

The elf lawyers huddled in alarm.

"I'm sorry, Mr. Claus," said Judge Thorne. "But I must turn this tape over to the DA's office. Bailiffs. Please take Mr. Claus into custody."

Two husky bailiffs marched over to Santa.

"But that's not me on the tape!"

"Your Honor," said Henry. "If Santa undergoes treatment and attends AA, I recommend his bail be reduced to—"

"Shut up, counselor."

Henry decided not to argue as the bailiffs dragged Santa away. Like a bratty Yank at Wimbledon, he'd just knocked his opponent off the court.

Thirty-Three

The giant sunglasses made him look like an alien, though they did hide the shame of his black eye. Walking in constant darkness, Junior felt like a faraway visitor at Planet Toys. Without a map, one could easily get lost in the winding maze of aisles.

After a nerve-racking journey through cymbal-banging monkeys, he finally wandered upon a shelf of action figures. Brutally designed, they probably looked nothing like the robot his father had once asked for.

"Can I help you find something?" said a tired old employee pushing a mop.

"I'm looking for Mr. Steely."

"Mr. Steely? Why, we stopped carrying those years ago."

"Could you order one for me?"

"I'm afraid they no longer make those, son."

"That's what I was afraid of," said Junior, leaving the store in disappointment.

Thirty-Four

If Santa's arrival in New York City hadn't been shocking enough, Trish was even more astounded to see him leaving the courthouse in handcuffs. Unable to find the remote, she scurried to the TV to turn up the volume. Reporters Patrick Carol and Carol Patrick were live on the scene for Action-7 News.

"What a shock to Santa's supporters out here today," said Patrick.

"And to boys and girls across the country," said Carol, turning to Santa as bailiffs led him past the shamefully quiet crowd. One after another, their SUPP♥RT SANTA signs went down like tumbling dominoes.

"Say it ain't so, Santa," cried a little boy.

"It ain't so," said Santa, quickly escorted away to leave many children in tears.

"Not since the fall of Shoeless Joe Jackson has America's youth been so tragically disappointed by one of their heroes."

"You're right, Patrick," said Carol. "Who the heck is Shoeless Joe?"

"A former ballplayer. He and his teammates were banned from the game after fixing the World Series in 1919."

"Oh. Well these children look like they've been hit with a bat."

Endless little faces were sobbing on the TV screen.

Trish numbly watched, unsure how she was going to tell Junior when he came tromping through the front door.

"Hey Mom, what's wrong?"

"Oh, well, your father just had Santa Claus arrested."

"What! What for?"

"Breaking and entering, among other things."

"You mean, he's calling Santa a burglar?"

Henry responded as a talking head on TV. "Once I'm done with the civil trial, I want to help our prosecutors make a case against Santa. . ."

Junior sadly watched. "I think I know what Dad's problem is."

"You do? Please share."

"Mr. Steely."

"Mr. Who?"

"It's a toy robot he never got as a child. And I'm gonna find out why." Still in coat and mittens, Junior headed back outside.

"Be home in time for dinner! And stay off—"

"The subway," said Junior, closing the door behind him.

Thirty-Five

As Junior headed off into the drizzly streets of New York, he vowed to make this Christmas special for his father. No more cheap colognes or stupid ties he would never wear.

Donning sunglasses, he strutted like an undercover cop in those endless detective shows. Already December, he had little time to solve two cases: One, finding out what his father had done to end up on Santa's naughty list; and two, to locate a Mr. Steely for him. Certainly, there was someone in this city of eight million who had tucked one away in a closet or attic.

With dusk approaching, Junior would have to take the subway if he was going to make it home in time for dinner. Breaking one rule to fulfill another, he tried to justify this reasoning, but could only wonder if Santa had godly powers of knowing and seeing all. If so, Santa would realize Junior was disobeying his mother by taking the dingy steps down to the C-train. As he vanished into the darkened underworld of the subway station, Junior feared Santa's naughty list far more than muggers or crazies.

Thirty-Six

Prisoner 459237 was Mr. Santa Claus in cell block 639C. Slumped over his cot in an orange prison jumpsuit, he looked more like a Halloween jack-o'-lantern than the bearded fat man who brought presents down the chimney.

His team of elf lawyers swarmed the dimly lit space. They were busy making phone calls and hacking away on mini-laptops.

"Our computers are running slow, Mr. Claus."

"Since they run on magnetic energy from the North Pole."

"We're just too far from home."

"But we're looking into your delivery at the Whitfield estate."

"To prove that surveillance tape is a fraud."

"I know it's a fraud! But how'd they get my glasses?" Santa raised an eyebrow over his trademark round frames.

The elves exchanged a puzzled look.

"You could've left them anywhere."

"Remember the time we found them in the Wheaties box?"

"Or when you left them in the freezer?"

"Or when Mrs. Claus found them in her panties drawer?"

The elves went silent from embarrassment. A plum-haired lawyer turned a deep shade of purple.

"Or maybe I really am getting senile," Santa said with a sigh.

"A little forgetful perhaps," said Mr. Elfsquire.

A burly guard opened the cell door and a harried little elf darted in. "We're still working on your bail, Mr. Claus. The Bank of Manhattan's having trouble with the exchange."

Thirty-Seven

That was an understatement in banking terms. Several flustered tellers had finally called on their manager to take over. A sexy professional with her own desk, she was just as baffled by the pile of sparkling coins. "I've never seen a magic elf coin before," she said to Mr. Elfrico, Santa's lawyer in charge of international exchanges.

World traveled, the handsome elf had encountered more women than his hero James Bond. At three feet tall, he had perfect view of the nametag on her busty chest. "Well, Tina," he said in a suavely high voice. "Allow me to demonstrate." Taking a coin from her hand, he turned it back and forth like a magician about to do a trick. "Heads is gold, tails silver." Sure enough, an elf's smiling face appeared on the gold side. A flip to silver revealed his cute little butt in tights.

"That's what's complicating the transaction. The ratio of gold to silver, and how to weigh the difference."

"I could explain it better over dinner tonight." Mr. Elfrico slyly pulled the coin from behind Tina's ear and slipped it back into her palm.

Judging by her bemused expression, his elf magic was already taking effect.

Thirty-Eight

Several hours had passed without any word from Mr. Elfrico. In the gloomy silence of Santa's cell, the elves' phones and computers had finally lost all magnetic charge from the North Pole. Though nobody said it, they were all beginning to wonder if they should've made this trip to New York.

"He's probably still working on the transaction," said Mr. Elfsquire.

"More likely, he's working on something else," said the plum-haired elf with blushing purple cheeks.

"He does like the ladies," said the rookie elf lawyer who'd dropped a dumbbell on his foot. The swelling had been wrapped with an Ace bandage long enough to mummify his entire body. Lucky for him, Santa's trainer had cut it down to elf proportions.

"We won't be seeing Mr. Elfrico again," said the chubby elf, his voice more envious than sad.

"It doesn't matter," said Santa from his cot. "This jail cell isn't much worse than the Pearly Gate Motel."

"It looked a lot better in the brochure," said the harried-looking elf who'd booked the reservation.

"Here comes the guard," said Mr. Elfsquire. "Maybe he has some news."

The guard's bald skull glistened beneath fluorescent lights. "You have a visitor, Mr. Claus," he said in a surprisingly gentle tone.

"Who is it?" said Santa.

"Is it the governor?" said Mr. Elfsquire. "Coming to give my client a pardon?"

"No. It's Henry Milton."

A stunned silence filled the narrow cell.

"What does he want?" said Santa. "To come rub salt in my wounds?"

"It's Henry Milton, Junior," said the guard.

"Oh, no. There's another one of those cretins on the loose?"

"He's just a little boy, sir. He seems pretty upset."

"All right. Let's see what he wants."

Thirty-Nine

They faced each other through a grimy window. Flying spittle had smeared the glass from previous phone conversations, not always happy ones in the dungeon-like prison.

"Have you been doing drugs, kid?"

"No. Why?"

"You're wearing sunglasses indoors."

"Oh," said Junior, taking off the shades. "I got beat up on the playground."

Santa winced at his puffy bruised eye. "Who did that to you?"

"Some punks at school. Are you gonna put them on your naughty list?"

"You didn't start the fight, did you?"

"No. I have the same name as my father."

Santa nodded sympathetically. "He should've hired bodyguards for you."

"Santa? Why didn't you bring him a Mr. Steely? That's all he ever wanted from you."

"Well," said Santa, extending the arms of his orange prison jumpsuit. "I think it's a fair guess to say he was on my naughty list."

"But he swears he was a good boy. That he was quiet and did his studies."

"Which led him to law school."

"He was all grown up by then."

"He must've done something as a boy that he's not telling."

"You don't remember?"

"Sorry, son. I deal with millions of kids each year, and that was a long time ago."

"But you'd remember someone like Jack the Ripper, right?"

"Your dad's not an axe murderer, if that's what you're asking."

"Good to know, but that doesn't help much." Junior glumly looked at Santa, who gave him a tender smile.

"You're a nice kid to be so concerned. If I ever get outta this joint, I'll bring you whatever toy you fancy."

"I don't want any toys."

"Then what would a boy your age want?"

"I want my parents back together."

Santa sighed helplessly into the phone. "I'm not God. Or Cupid. I can only bring toys and candy and baseball cards."

Junior sadly nodded. "Guess I was asking for a miracle."

"Sorry, kid, but I'm barely a saint."

"It's okay, Santa. Have a merry Christmas." Junior hung up the phone and retreated through the tough crowd of the visitors' center.

Santa regretfully watched him leave.

Forty

Smelling of mold, the thrift store was a sacred ground for lost artifacts. Tired of playing detective, Junior had found an Indiana Jones hat with a price tag of five bucks. Putting it on with some apprehension of lice, he reminded himself that treasure hunters had to survive the worst of nature's elements. Lice, bugs, or other creepy-crawly creatures might even become a source of protein in the wild.

In danger of being grounded, he checked the clock on the wall and hoped it was the one thing there in present time. Hustling down the cluttered aisles, he passed a messy pile of magazines, ranging from *Time* to *Newsweek* to *Life*, their months and years scrambled recklessly together, so that one might think Roosevelt launched the Space Shuttle, Marilyn copied Madonna, Nixon led the teardown of the Berlin Wall.

Along a dusty shelf was a stack of vinyl records. Lionel Ritchie, who-ever that was, had a big afro on his fading album cover. Motley Crew, Kool & the Gang, Kenny Rogers, all scratched up and forgotten.

And finally there were toys in a cardboard box—the cheap dark coffin for the vomit-stained teddy bears, the amputated Barbies and GI Joes. Digging through limbs and loose parts, Junior felt something metallic. A miniature robot!

Pulled from the remains, Mr. Steely came to view in full light. After years of neglect, he was now Mr. Rusty. Corrosion had eaten away his left eye and made his joints unbendable. A push of his voice command button produced nothing more than a dry, empty click.

Nothing a little oil couldn't fix, thought Junior, twisting Mr. Steely's head that broke off in his hand. "Oops! I'm sorry, Mr. Steely." Sadly he lowered the veteran robot into its box, careful to rest head on body for eternity.

Sorry Dad is what Junior was really feeling. On his way out of the store, he hung the Indiana Jones hat on its rack. So much for playing treasure hunter or detective. With his mother's dinner awaiting him, Junior would hurry home as Little Boy Blue.

Forty-One

Santa didn't return to his cell until after a prison cafeteria meal of Salisbury steak and instant mashed potatoes. Not too surprisingly, the meal was better than what room service normally provided at the Pearly Gate Motel.

As the door clanked shut behind him, he was surprised to see his elf lawyers busily working on new laptops.

"We got some hot new Apples, sir."

"From that Mac store across the street."

"And believe it or not, they're totally compatible with our software!"

"We're starting a background check on the B-B Twins."

"Blaire and Blaine," said Mr. Elfsquire. "I wouldn't be surprised if those two were on your naughty list."

"Which means you never would've entered the Whitfield—"

"That can wait," said Santa. "Find me the file on Henry Milton—Senior."

"Getting some dirt on your opponent, sir?"

"I just want the truth about this guy." Santa took a seat on the cot and kicked off his boots.

"Sure thing, Mr. Claus." A flurry of little fingers typed away. Within seconds, the elves downloaded photos and data of Henry Milton's life, starting with an adorable baby picture, and leading up to his days in a slick lawyer's suit.

"Henry Milton, Senior."

"Born at Saint Vincent's Hospital in New York City."

"Attended Public School Number 27 in the Bronx."

"Model student, Boy Scout, volunteer."

"Gave his lunch money to kids with less money."

"Even though he was poor."

"Dirt poor."

"But never complained."

"Just worked hard and made the best of it."

"Until the third grade."

Turning silent, the elves exchanged a nervous look.

"What happened?" said Santa.

"He stopped believing in you, sir."

"When you neglected to bring him a Mr. Steely."

Santa frowned at their computers. "How did such a fine young man end up on my naughty list?"

"Don't blame technology, sir," said Mr. Elfsquire. "Our software system had him ranked at the top of your list."

"He was 97.6 percent good boy."

"Took a peek at his Dad's *Playboy* once."

"But with Miss Brazil on the cover, what boy wouldn't?"

The elves nodded in unison, the plum-haired one blushing so brightly his face resembled a grape.

"Then how could I have forgotten him?" said Santa.

"Let's see," said Mr. Elfsquire, as the elves searched their computers for more answers:

"Says here a Mr. Steely was loaded onto your sleigh at nineteen-hundred hours."

"And you arrived at his neighborhood at twenty-one-thirty, Eastern Standard Time."

"With deliveries made to every house on the block."

"Except Henry Milton's."

"I just don't understand," said an utterly baffled Santa.

From down the corridor marched heavy footsteps. A shiny reflection warned of the bald guard approaching.

"You finally made bail, Mr. Claus."

"It's about time," said Mr. Elfsquire, clearly unhappy with his lawyer in charge of international 'exchanges.'

"Better late than never," said Santa, putting his boots back on. "I won't rest until we find out what happened to that Mr. Steely."

Forty-Two

Buzzing on his second glass of champagne, Henry had already forgotten the name of the yuppie Manhattan bar that Nora had dragged him into. Seated at a candlelit table in the back, they raised a bubbly toast. "To exposing the biggest fraud since Milli Vanilli," said Henry.

"Who's that?" Nora said blankly.

Henry suddenly felt the fourteen years between them. "They were this Top Forty group back in the day. Couple of guys in dreadlocks who sang and danced and won a Grammy for this really stupid song."

"Big surprise," said Nora, who was way too hip to listen to pop music.

"Yeah. Turns out they were lip-syncing and couldn't even carry a tune. Had to give their Grammy back and apologize to all their fans."

Nora chuckled. "Well nobody's going to forget Santa. Or the lawyer who did him in." They clanked glasses a bit too hard, spilling champagne onto a spread of tabloids. Endless headlines and photos showed the NAUGHTY SANTA CAUGHT ON TAPE.

"Today they found out he's a drunk and a burglar," said Henry. "Wait until they discover he's a womanizer and an abuser."

"He beats his little elves?"

"No, but he maims kids with his toys. That said, I'm hoping to settle this thing before Christmas."

"That'd be perfect. We could spend the holiday in Spain. I know of the perfect little villa."

"Oh. I sort of promised Junior I'd be watching him open presents."

"Aren't you going to see him tonight?"

"Yeah," said Henry, checking his watch. He'd promised to take him shopping for his mother in another hour or so.

"Come on, Henry. With Santa out of the picture, Christmas no longer means what it used to."

Henry stared at Santa's photo with troubled thoughts. "If only he'd given me that Mr. Steely."

"But he didn't. Because 'Saint' Nick is really just a despot."

Henry nodded and gulped his champagne like a cowboy in a whiskey saloon. Slamming his glass down, he wiped his mouth with the back of his hand. "Beware Santa. I'm ready for our final showdown."

Nora smiled and wrangled him in for a kiss.

Forty-Three

"Maybe we should've taken the sleigh," said Santa, as another taxi whizzed by without stopping. For the past twenty minutes, he and his elves had been standing along the curb, waving their arms like fools at every cabbie to pass by.

"Nowhere to park it anyway," said Mr. Elfsquire, keeping his eye on approaching headlights. "And besides, the reindeer get too jumpy with all this noise." A blaring horn made them jump back in fright. In a flash of a New York second, the headlights became taillights that sped off without them.

"This city's makin' me dizzy," said Santa. "Too many lights, too many people, too many cars—all going in completely opposite directions."

To their surprise, a taxi came ripping to a stop. The driver wore a handsome turban and spoke in a sing-song accent that made the elves want to dance: "Are you the real Santa Claus? Not some two-bit imposter?"

"Ho-ho-ho. And what's your name, Mr. Driver?"

"Jiva Baksheesh. And you did not bring a present to my little Bansi." A turn of the visor revealed a photo of his son. Like his daddy, he had big brown eyes that peered out from his turban.

"Cute kid," said Santa.

"Cute kid with no presents," said the cabbie.

"But Mr. Baksheesh? Does your family even celebrate Christmas?"

"That does not matter! You are a racist bastard, Mr. Claus, and I'm going to hire Henry Milton to sue your sorry ass!" Tearing off in a blur of yellow, his tires splattered mud onto Santa and his elves.

"What is wrong with people in this country?" Santa tried wiping the grime off his red and white suit, only to smear it in.

"Screw it," said the rookie elf lawyer. "If they don't stop, I'm suing." He jumped in front of the next approaching cab and flailed his arms. In a skid of burning rubber, the cab screeched to a halt, just inches from the miniature lawyer.

"Ho-ho-ho." Santa and his elves piled in, ready to journey forth in their quest for Mr. Steely.

Forty-Four

An experienced New Yorker like Henry had far less trouble hailing a taxi. Now in his fourth cab in the past half hour, he was zigzagging across town in hopes of losing the paparazzi. Like mobsters with cameras, they'd been waiting to jump him as he'd left the restaurant with a goodbye kiss to Nora.

"It's not easy being famous," he told the driver, a faceless beard who only grunted, probably not understanding a word of English. "Might be different if I were a Broadway actor or played for the Knicks. But I'm not someone people look up to."

The driver didn't argue as he tore through a light turning red.

Henry stopped talking and watched the crowded sidewalks outside. Very few of these people wanted an autograph or photo taken with the lawyer who'd single-handedly decanonized a saint. For countless generations, Saint Nick had represented love and peace and charity to these folks. With his white beard, chubby belly and twinkling eyes, he was everybody's grandfather, that kindly old man who brought Christmas cheer.

But now Henry was telling them otherwise.

As they turned down Broadway, he spotted two boys with the Superman "S" on their jackets. Sprinting ahead of their family, they leapt over the curb with arms spread to fly. Henry chuckled. Deep down, every man wanted to shed his Clark Kent glasses to be something more. Perhaps that is why the vast majority would rather not know the human dark side of their heroes. For instance, John Wayne never performed his own action scenes, but left the Indian killing to stunt doubles and camera tricks. FDR kept a mistress while leading his nation through Depression and war. George Washington never cut down a cherry tree. Abe Lincoln may have recruited unregistered voters. The list went on and on, but Santa was far more sacred than politicians or cowboy film stars. Taking down Saint Nick was like taking down the Pope, a figure given godly powers by tradition and need.

No wonder the world should despise Henry. Like a foolish prank in chemistry class, he had conjured Santa from the sky, only to watch his experiment blow up in their faces.

"Keep driving," he told the cabbie. On his way to pick up his son, he would soon brave the masses at Rockefeller Plaza to go Christmas shopping.

Forty-Five

Unbeknownst to both Santa and Henry, they briefly crossed paths at the intersection of 120th and Broadway. Miraculously, there was no collision between their two cabs.

Piled up in the backseat, the elf lawyers were crushing Santa's knees, making him wonder how the department store Santas endured the long line of kids wanting their pictures taken in "Dear Santa's" lap.

At a sudden red light they came to a jarring stop, the elves flying up like ping pong balls that caromed off the seats, windows and ceiling. "Oof!" "Oof!" "Oof!"

Torn from Santa's lap, they landed in a clumsy tangle on the floorboards, leaving Santa to freely gaze outside the window. On the sidewalk was a scrawny Jamaican selling trinkets. Spread over his colorful blanket were miniature Statues of Liberty.

"Remember that time I almost flew straight into her torch?"

The elves crawled up on the seat to peer outside.

"It was foggy that night, Mr. Claus."

"And Rudolph was out with the flu."

"But you still showed amazing reflexes, sir."

"Otherwise, we'd've been calling the Coast Guard."

The elves shivered at the thought of the icy Atlantic.

"We were lucky," said Santa, "but Mr. Steely could've fallen out on that hard turn."

"Wrong year," said Mr. Elfsquire, first to open his laptop for data.

"Perhaps a bird carried it away. Damn seagulls."

"Unlikely, Mr. Claus. They usually go for the gummy bears."

"Wait! Was that the year I slipped on that icy rooftop and almost broke my neck? Could've easily fallen out of my bag."

"Right year," said the chubby elf with a punch of his Enter key. "But that was on the Hovdes' rooftop in Minnesota."

Santa sighed in frustration.

"Yo Santa!" said the scruffy driver, his eyes peering into the rearview mirror. "You check beneath your seats?"

"Well, no, I only take the sleigh out once a year."

"Every Christmas, I find all kinds 'a stuff wedged down there. From teddy bears to lingerie. Heck, I barely gotta go shoppin' for the fam."

The elves raised their fuzzy little eyebrows at the possibility.

"Take us back to the Pearly Gate Motel," said Santa.

The cabbie tore off into traffic. "I owe ya one, Santa. For the time you got me 'dat Luke Skywalker action figure. My parents never could've afforded 'dat."

"You deserved it, Tony."

"Aw shucks, ya even remembered my name." Beaming with pride, Tony had no idea Santa had just read his name off the cab license pinned to his dash.

Forty-Six

A December evening in the Rockefeller Plaza! Where darkness is only a backdrop for Christmas lights everywhere. From heaven, they might appear as painted snowdrops wafting over the rink of skaters. How they whirl in perfect harmony, scarves and hair whipping in a cold breeze, whiffs of cookies and roasted nuts stirring appetites. A horse-drawn carriage passes by with a handsome couple in the back. Noses red from cold, they snuggle together like a prince and princess.

Stepping out of this winter fairy tale are two guys from the Bronx wearing sunglasses at night. Born of the same name, the larger one is hoping to hide his face from paparazzi and hostile observers. The smaller one is covering a black eye from a playground rumble. If not for the Macy's bags strapped over their arms, these two characters might pass as tough guys.

"I hope Mom likes this perfume," said Junior, sniffing the fancy little box with the French name he couldn't pronounce.

"It's always been her favorite," said Henry, keeping a careful watch on the crowd.

"She smells nice, huh Dad?"

"Well, she doesn't stink. Except for her breath in the morning, but don't tell 'er I said that."

"It's okay. She says the closet still reeks from your old running shoes."

"She said that? My feet don't stink!"

Junior said nothing in response.

"They don't. Do they?"

"She never wanted to hurt your feelings."

"Yeah, well nobody else has complained."

They walked in silence past a lingerie shop.

"And who's that nobody, Dad?"

"Nobody."

"So she's not that important to ya, huh?"

Henry pretended not to hear as they approached a jewelry store. The sparkle of power and lust allured them to the window. On display was a regal set of diamond earrings, necklace and bracelet.

"Wow!" said Junior. "Those look like the crown jewels."

"Yeah," said Henry with a cautious look at the price tag.

"You were right about Santa, Dad."

"I was?"

"He can't bring me what I want. Only you can."

"That's right, buddy. Anything you want."

"How 'bout this necklace for Mom?"

"You got expensive tastes, kiddo."

"Does that mean you'll get it for her?"

Henry slowly nodded, surprised by his somber reflection in the glass.

"Once I settle this case, I might be able to loan you—"

"I don't want to borrow anything. I think you should give it to her."

"Oh, I think she'd be happy to get it from you." Henry led Junior away from the window.

"Dad? Don't you think Mom is prettier than that lady you're seeing?"

"Her name's Nora, and I don't think we should—"

"I bet ya Mom's a lot nicer."

"Junior, this really isn't—"

"And nobody makes better meatloaf than Mom."

"True, but Nora doesn't cook."

"See—don't tell me you don't miss those Sunday night dinners."

"Well," Henry confessed, "Your mom's meatloaf was always my favorite."

"She hasn't made it since you left."

"Really?"

"She hardly ever makes dinners like she used to."

"I'm sorry to hear that. Don't tell me you're stuck eating chili dogs?"

"And instant macaroni."

"Ugggh!" They both made the same disgusted face and sound.

"Well, after I hit the jackpot with this lawsuit, I'll make sure you and your mom are eating prime rib every night."

"But are you gonna be there too?" Junior gazed up at his father with a pleading look.

"I'm always gonna be there for ya, Junior. But not with you and your mom."

Junior exhaled a cloudy breath. "So I can't believe in you or Santa."

Henry started to say something but couldn't find the words.

Father and son walked in anguished silence.

Forty-Seven

Up on the rooftop of the Pearly Gate Motel, the reindeer grew antsy beneath a full moon. Fat and yellow, it hung from the sky like a neon ball. No need for flashlights, Santa and his elves frantically inspected the sleigh for Mr. Steely.

Digging beneath the seats, they had so far discovered endless candy bar wrappers, a petrified slice of pizza, and a McDonald's bag of stale fries.

"Ho-ho-ho. I'll never forget the look on that poor kid's face in the drive-thru."

The elves cracked up laughing.

"That cop in front of us nearly choked on his Big Mac."

"It's no wonder they screwed up our order."

"I asked for extra pickles."

"And I said no onions."

"They forgot my hot apple turnover," said the chubby elf.

"Maybe not," said Mr. Elfsquire, holding up a shriveled black pastry covered in mold.

"Must've dropped it down the seat," said the chubby elf in grave disappointment.

"At least we know what was making that smell," said the rookie plugging his nose.

"Hang on," said Santa, reaching down into the crevice between the arm rest and driver's seat. "I feel something metal . . . this could be it." He yanked out a diet soda can to everyone's disappointment.

In the back of the sleigh, the chubby elf crawled headfirst beneath the seat, his little butt sticking up with the crack showing. In a muffled voice, he called out: "Wait! I think this might be it!" Squirming out from the crawlspace, he appeared with messy hair and glasses titled sideways to present "Mr. Steely!"

"Ooooooooooh!" The elves gathered around in wonder.

Santa solemnly took the toy robot and read its tag: "To Henry, Love Santa." Looking up, his face showed deep regrets. "One little mistake and I created a monster."

"Make that two, sir!" The plum-haired elf popped up with an old wooden doll from the eighteenth century. "This one was for Napoleon."

"Glad to know it wasn't short man's complex," said Mr. Elfsquire.

"Poor little Napoleon," said the chubby elf.

"Poor little Henry," said Santa. "I can't imagine how badly he must've felt."

The elves sadly nodded. A heavy silence weighed over them, as if that hefty moon might plop down on their heads.

Forty-Eight

Some might say the "collective unconscious" is nothing more than a silly theory by the dreamers like Carl Jung. But dreamers are everywhere, and tonight, an unlikely trio was tapped into the same invisible wire. Tossing and turning in three separate lodgings, Henry, Junior and Santa were rocking-'n-rolling in complete harmony to an Elvis Presley tune:

"Are You Lonesome Tonight?" sang Santa so loudly it woke him with a start. "Elvis?" he called out in a puzzled voice, rubbing sleep from his eyes in his darkened motel room.

Surprisingly, the elves remained snoring in their rollaway cots. Careful not to wake them, Santa crept toward the window in his nightgown. Scattered in its pockets were special keepsakes from over the years. His favorite was an old black-and-white photo of his wife in a bikini. Taken during their honeymoon in the south of France, she was quite the little doozy.

In another pocket was a St. Christopher medallion. Sent by an Italian boy during World War II, it was intended to keep Santa safe from warplanes buzzing the sky. Proven effective, Santa was standing here now, sad to know that Mr. Federico Mancini had grown up to die of a heart attack. Decades after the war, he was cheering on his country at the World's Cup when he doubled over from sudden cardiac arrest. Needless to say, Italians take their soccer very seriously.

Stashed deeper in Santa's pocket was a letter that even his wife knew nothing about. Opened several times, its yellowing creases were beginning to wear. Postmarked December 12, 1942 from Tupelo, Mississippi, the sender must've been in the second or third grade:

Dear Santa:

All I want for Christmas is a guitar. Someday, I hope to bring rhythm and blues to white people.

Yours truly,

Elvis Presley

P.S. Momma says sorry for the butterscotch cookies; they got burned a little but still taste good with milk.

Santa finished reading the letter in the glow of moonlight. Every Christmas, he grappled with the "what ifs?" surrounding Elvis. Had Santa not brought him the guitar, Elvis may have never been heard of, instead becoming a cotton farmer or insurance salesman who only sang in his church choir. While the rest of the world may have lost out on his shaking hips and lip-curled singing, Elvis may have been spared from a tragic life that ended much too soon.

Be careful what you wish for. Santa folded up the letter and put it back in its envelope. Gazing out the window, he whispered softly upon a star, "That goes for you too, Henry Milton. And Henry Milton, Junior."

Forty-Nine

Morning daylight bleached the moon from the sky. Before the coffee shops were even open, Patrick Carol and Carol Patrick arrived on the courthouse steps with their Action-7 News crew. Deprived of caffeine, they joined a dwindling group of Santa's supporters. Huddled together, the Faithful Dozen held up signs: WE STILL BELIEVE!

"With Santa against the ropes," said Patrick, "we prepare for day three of trial."

"And as you can see," said Carol, "his public support has quickly faded." She greeted a tough Bronx woman by shoving a microphone in her face. "Good morning, ma'am. I see you still believe in the man in the red suit?"

"You bet your ass! I don't believe for one second 'dat tape was for real!"

"That's right!" said a beefy construction worker. "And even if it was, nobody's perfect!"

"Not even Santa!" said a little girl hugging her teddy bear.

"Besides," said a uniformed ambulance driver. "He's got a stressful job!"

"Delivering millions of packages overnight? Who wouldn't sneak a sip now and then?" A Parcels-Express driver took a swig off a thermos smelling of Irish coffee.

"Amen!" shouted a ruddy-faced priest to spark a cheer from the Faithful Dozen waving signs.

Standing before them, the two reporters smiled.

"That just might be a good defense, Patrick."

"You're right, Carol. And Santa could use all the help he can get today."

Fifty

For the first time in his twenty years on the bench, Judge Thorne had reluctantly allowed TV cameras into his courtroom. A phone call from the President of the United States had definitely influenced the former naval commander's decision. Even though Judge Thorne hadn't voted for the draft-dodging cowboy, he still respected the man's rank. And if the Commander-in-Chief wanted to watch "The Santa Suit" on TV, he would do so, with millions of others across the globe.

The Patriot News Network (PNN) warmed the stage for Henry by showing a retired Hall of Famer endorsing a male performance drug, followed by commercials for ladies' fresh deodorant, kiss-worthy toothpaste, and antacids to combat everything from greasy pizza to spicy chili dogs.

Finally making his grand appearance, Henry became an instant star in people's living rooms. Dressed in a silk gray suit, he glimmered beneath the camera lights like a knight in shining armor. Leading an army of expert witnesses, Sir Henry fought to defend the honor of children everywhere, including Max Wheeler in his purple Mohawk and matching arm cast.

According to Federal Safety Commissioner Ron E. Bullard, "a faulty weld most certainly resulted in the wheel coming off the boy's skateboard."

"Thereby resulting in a fractured wrist," stated Dr. Melvin Prattle with expert authority on impact injuries.

"Such childhood trauma will likely cause permanent psychological damage," attested Dr. T.P. Cummings, dean of psychiatry at Fordham University.

"All this talk is making me hungry," shrilled Bradley Truffle to his mother in the plaintiff's row. As if by request, Channel 23 cut to a string of commercials for fast food burgers, a new minty shake for the holiday season, swirly elf cookies, and puppy dog chow. For those weighing more than a Saint Bernard, a weight loss clinic was already offering its New Year's special to burn off those Christmas calories.

Returning to trial, Henry called a team of forensic scientists to the stand. With godlike authority, they linked Santa's fingerprints to a plate of chocolate chip cookies in the Sheepshanks' living room. Since Shelly's saliva had washed Santa's prints from her jawbreaker, they could only present circumstantial evidence to prove it had in fact come from Mr. Claus.

"Clearly Santa was in the house," concurred private investigator and retired police officer Sam Sampson.

"I never said I wasn't," grumbled Santa to his elf lawyers in the defense row.

"They're turning this into a criminal investigation," replied the rookie elf.

"More like a witch hunt," said Mr. Elfsquire with an appalled frown.

"Those cookies were never even for Santa," Shelly Sheepshank testified. "They were for my Granny coming to visit."

Fifty-One

For the majority of TV viewers, circumstances alone were enough. After witnessing the tape of a drunken Santa burglarizing the Whitfields' home, they had already made up their minds. Santa Claus was guilty. Betrayed and united, they rooted for Henry to destroy, destroy, destroy!

For every legal bomb Henry dropped, Santa's elf lawyers retaliated with the force of a cap gun. Following a hemorrhoidal cream ad, Mr. Elfsquire called Shelly Sheepshank to the stand for cross examination. Through the gaps in her mouth, she sprayed him with her statement: "A jawbreaker's s'posed to break your jaw, not your teeth."

Santa watched in disgust. "Next thing ya know, they'll be calling in a linguistics expert."

A stuffy professor from Columbia University proved him correct. "As a leading authority in my field, I tend to agree that the term 'jawbreaker' is in fact misleading."

After a longwinded lecture on semantics, Judge Thorne ordered a recess to use the restroom. During this lengthy break, the Golden Years Network (GYN) appropriately aired commercials for bran cereals, gentle laxatives, and geriatric supplements. When Judge Thorne finally returned to the bench with a relieved smile, one might have mistaken him as another elderly actor in the sequence of ads.

"Let's continue with cross examination," he announced with less strain in his voice.

Moments later, Mr. Elfsquire questioned Max Wheeler on the stand. "According to your medical report, you rode your skateboard off a forty-foot ramp while attempting to jump over a line of cars."

"So? That doesn't mean the wheel should come off."

"Well, in that case, have you considered jumping off the Grand Canyon?"

"Objection!" shouted Henry, to steal a reverse angle from the news cameras.

"Sustained!" said Judge Thorne, unsure which camera to look at. By the time he figured it out, they had already swiveled back to Max Wheeler responding:

"No. But that would be totally rad, little elf dude."

Rising laughter echoed off the courtroom walls. Without realizing it, the live audience was turning the trial into a sitcom. Part comedy, part courtroom thriller, "The Santa Suit" was by far the most entertaining show on the tube.

Fifty-Two

In Times Square, thousands gathered like a swarm of ants at the toes of King Kong. Instead of gazing up at a massive gorilla, they witnessed the largest pair of breasts in the history of mankind. Appearing on the Sony Jumbotron was Rene Reno. Hair dyed platinum blonde, she wore dark-red lipstick on a mouth moving with captions across the forty-foot screen: "Santa came tiptoeing into my bedroom and asked me to sit in his lap."

Loud cheers arose from an NYU fraternity. "Let's go put on some red suits and beards and try that back at the girls' dorms!" High-fiving one another, they took off through the crowd of enthralled viewers.

* * *

"And why did you sit in his lap?" Henry asked Rene in the courtroom.

"Because I trusted him. After all, he is Santa Claus."

"So you didn't know he was just a dirty old man?"

Santa jumped to his feet before his lawyers could object. "I don't even remember you, lady!"

"See! I'm just another notch on his belt," cried Rene, bursting into tears. "I'll never trust another man again!"

Santa quickly sat down, trying to ignore the dirty glares from the females in attendance. Even Carol Patrick, notorious for her "unbiased reporting," looked ready to strangle him with her microphone cord.

Among the horde of angry faces, there was one woman smiling: Nora Powers, who could've kissed Henry and Santa both.

Fifty-Three

The Faithful Dozen remained outside the courthouse. On their six-inch TV, Rene Reno was reduced to a small, fragile woman. Even her triple-D breasts appeared as baby watermelons, much too young and ripe for a man Santa's age.

"Pervert," said the ambulance driver.

"Womanizer," said the tough Bronx woman.

"To think of 'em cheating on Mrs. Claus," said the ruddy-faced priest.

Dropping their signs, Santa's last supporters walked away.

Fifty-Four

Trish was trying to finish her angel sculpture but was distracted by things not so angelic on TV.

"And then he offered me a new toy," said Rene Reno. "And it wasn't the kind you see at Planet Toys."

Judge Thorne, perhaps not knowing Channel 12's camera was on him, was lustily staring at Miss Reno's bare thighs. "Did it come with batteries?"

Trish quickly turned down the volume as Junior entered the room. "Hey sweetie, this may not be for kids."

"For all I care, Dad and Santa can both go jump in the East River." Junior grabbed a puzzle book from the table and retreated to his room.

Trish watched him in concern. In just a few minutes, she would go talk to her troubled little boy. But even in New York, where everyone was an actor—whether on a Broadway stage or not—it was never easy for a single mother to play the role of father.

Fifty-Five

Henry put Saint Nick on the stand as a false idol to be struck down.

"Did you or did you not harass my client in her bedroom?"

"If I did something to upset her, I am truly sorry."

"You should be, Mr. Claus."

Rene Reno sobbed hysterically in the plaintiff's row. Unlike Trish, she was a horrible actress who believed she was worthy of a Tony Award.

Santa was clearly annoyed by her performance. "How much will it take to shut her up?"

"Money is not the issue here," said Henry.

"A million dollars!" exclaimed Rene Reno. "To pay for my pain and suffering!"

Santa shook his head in disgust. "And what about the rest of your clients? And those thousands of others in line?"

"Are you finally ready to settle?" said Henry, barely able to contain the excitement in his voice.

"I'm ready to retire."

The audience gasped in surprise.

The old school journalists quickly jotted Santa's quote.

"Your Honor!" said Mr. Elfsquire. "May I have a word with my client?"

"There's nothing more to discuss," said Santa. "It's time to sell off the toy factory. As I'm sure you know, Mr. Milton, it's worth a pretty penny."

"Several billion! And I'm sure the major toy companies would be eager to make an offer!"

"So long as Mrs. Claus and I have enough to retire in the Caribbean. And my elves are well provided for."

"Of course, of course!"

The plaintiff's row erupted like the winning dugout of the World Series. Rene Reno hugged her triple D's against a delighted Mr. Sheepshank. His daughter Shelly danced in the aisle with the B-B Twins, while Mr. and Mrs. Whitfield triumphantly shook hands with Nora. For the first time in months, Bradley Truffle whistled on purpose to the joy of his mother's ears. Yelling over him, Max Wheeler raised his arm cast in victory. "ALLLLLLL RIGHT, DUDES!"

Judge Thorne hammered his gavel over the commotion. "Let's schedule a hearing for tomorrow morning."

"Yes, your Honor," said Santa. "But first I'd like to apologize to all the boys and girls out there who will now go without toys."

A smattering of children broke into sobs. After Rene Reno's X-rated testimony, they finally understood what was going on.

Santa sadly gazed down on them. "The reason I started this business was to help families in need."

"Sure it was," mumbled Henry.

"And that's why I owe you a big apology." Santa stepped down from the stand to approach Henry. Reaching into his red suit coat, he presented Mr. Steely. "This was meant for you years and years ago. I'm sorry it's so late, and I'm sorry for the problems I may have caused you."

Dumbfounded, Henry accepted the little robot and read its tag: "To Henry, Love Santa." Eyes misting, he looked up at Santa and cleared his throat. "I—I—I don't understand."

"It fell down beneath the seat of my sleigh."

"With the McDonald's fries," said the chubby elf with a hungry expression.

Henry slowly nodded in understanding. "Thank you, Santa."

Santa gave him a loving smile. "You were a good boy, Henry. And I still have high hopes for you."

"You do?"

"It's easy to make mistakes. The hard part is forgiving."

Listening carefully, Henry clung to his robot with a boyish innocence.

From the plaintiff's row, Nora and his clients nervously watched, their stomachs unsettling from a magnetic shift in the courtroom, one that only could have arisen from the North Pole.

PART THREE

SURRENDER

One

Staying true to her role of mother, Trish brought her son a steaming cup of hot chocolate. "You can't keep blaming your father for the divorce."

Seated at his desk, Junior was connecting the dots in his puzzle book. "That's not what you told Aunt Reggie on the phone."

"Okay, so maybe it was ninety percent his fault, but I could be a witch on days that weren't Halloween."

"Why is Dad chasing a hot piece of ass?"

Trish was momentarily stunned into silence. "You really need to stop listening in to my phone conversations."

"What did you mean by that?"

"A lot of men go for younger women after they get divorced."

"I think you have a hotter ass than her, Mom."

Trish smiled and mussed Junior's hair. "Thanks, sweetie. You'll make a fine husband someday."

And hopefully a better father than Henry Senior, she said silently to herself.

Two

A media frenzy chased Henry out of the courthouse. Leading the pack were Patrick Carol and Carol Patrick.

"Mr. Milton! What kind of settlement are you expecting?"

"Well—I just want my clients to get what they deserve."

"And what would that be?"

Henry stared blankly into their TV cameras. "I'll need to think about that." Down the steps he escaped with Mr. Steely in hand.

Right behind him was Nora, busting through the throng of reporters. "Henry! Let's go celebrate!"

"I dunno. I kinda got a headache."

"Nothing a good martini couldn't fix."

"Maybe later." Henry stayed two steps ahead of her, almost slipping on an icy patch.

"Santa was playing you in there, Henry. Don't start getting soft on 'em now!"

"Yeah," Henry said unconvincingly. "I probably just need some fresh air." He pushed through another band of reporters and headed off alone.

"He's just a stupid robot toy!" Nora called after him.

Henry glanced back and waved Mr. Steely in the air.

Three

Several blocks ahead, Henry walked Riverside Drive, named appropriately for its cobblestone path along the Hudson, its streaming waters darkened by the reflection of rain clouds.

Lost in a flow of thoughts, Henry had stopped thinking somewhere near Columbus Circle. Wherever he was heading, he wasn't even sure. An inner force was now driving him forward instead of decisive reasoning or strategy.

Passing a playground, he was taken from his meditative state by a group of children playing. A little girl in a dingy jacket ran up to her mother. "Is it true, Mommy? The kids at school say there's no more Santa."

"He's just getting old and tired, honey."

Henry watched the girl sobbing in her mother's arms. Slipping past them, he hid Mr. Steely behind his back.

Four

Still half-dazed, Henry didn't even remember the subway ride from Manhattan to the Bronx. Crossing his childhood schoolyard, he unknowingly approached the punks who had beaten up Junior.

Their ringleader Darren was trying to swallow a magic elf whistle, but kept choking it up. "I need some help gettin' this down," he snarled at his friends gathered round. "I could really use a million bucks!"

A thuggish boy drew a long narrow comb. "I want fifty thousand."

"Twenty-five," bargained Darren.

"Thirty and I'll shove 'dat whistle so far down your t'roat you'll never talk right again."

"Okay, you got a—"

The deal was closed with a violent gag.

Watching in bewilderment, Henry circled past them before they could ask him to be their lawyer.

Five

Trish put a bow and price tag on her finished winged bust. The largest of her pieces, her angel guarded over the snowman, skaters, and Nutcracker soldier, which better served ballet than military prowess. Beneath the Christmas tree lights, her exhibit glowed with a magical beauty.

A frantic buzzing on the intercom was hopefully a customer responding to her ad in *The Little Merchant* newspaper.

"Hello!" said Trish into the speaker. "Are you here for my sculptures?"

"Trish! It's me!" squawked Henry's voice.

"Oh. Guess not then." Unable to hide her disappointment, she buzzed Henry into the building with a push of the button.

Moments later, he would materialize out of thin air like something out of *Star Trek* or a vampire movie, preferably not the latter. Standing behind her, Henry quietly admired her growing art display.

"That's really amazing."

Trish turned to see if he was being sincere. "Since when did you become a fan of my work?"

"What do you mean?"

"You used to say my 'hobby' took up the entire living room. Kept you from having a recliner and a big screen."

Henry took a closer look at her works, clearly impressed by the minute details of carving. "I'd like to buy a few of these. How much for the fairy?"

"Angel, remember? And I don't accept charity."

"It's not charity. Your work has really taken off."

"It took off right beneath your nose. You just never took the time to notice."

Henry regretfully nodded. "I'd buy them all if I could."

"Plllllease. You're about to settle the biggest class action in history."

Henry shrugged. "Where's Junior? I've got something to show 'em." He proudly held up his shiny toy robot.

"He's in his room," said Trish with a bemused smile. "And he's not doing so well with the divorce. Our first Christmas apart, ya know."

"Maybe Mr. Steely and I can cheer 'em up." Marching off like a robot, Henry proceeded toward Junior's door that was marked by a poster of a handsome Yankees player.

Trish watched Henry as if a stranger had entered the apartment. "Have you been drinking, Henry?"

"No, ma'am."

"Then what's gotten into you?"

"I've got a new toy."

Six

Junior's door burst open with the force of a tropical storm. Hurricane Henry, to be precise. "Look what Santa gave me!"

"Yeah," said Junior, barely glancing up from his puzzle book at his father's metal contraption.

Henry spoke in a mechanical robot voice: "My-name-is Mis-ter Stee-ly and your fath-er says I-can-stay-with-you when-ever you-want."

"That's nice, but you can tell my dad I'm too old for toys now. Thanks to his 'tough lessons' in life." Junior concentrated on an illustrated brain-teaser, trying to figure out how many rectangular kites would fit into a measured square.

"Need some help with that?"

"I need to do things on my own. Remember?"

Henry sighed in response. "I wasted a lot'a years being angry with my father."

"Why? Your father actually stuck around."

"When he wasn't getting drunk at the bowling alley."

"At least he didn't leave your mom for a hot piece of ass."

"Where'd you hear that?! Was your mom talking to Aunt Reggie?"

Junior reluctantly nodded.

"Should've known."

* * *

Ear pressed to Junior's door, Trish was eavesdropping on their conversation. Suddenly she realized her face was right on the crotch of the Yankees poster boy. With a whispered apology, she scooted a few inches over to hear Henry say:

"I never left your mother for another woman."

Trish smiled, glad to hear that little tramp was nothing more than a rebound.

"We all make mistakes," Henry continued. "God knows I've made my fair share with you and your mom."

"At least you finally admit it," Trish said loud enough to blow her cover. Before she could retreat down the hall, the door flew open and she fell into Henry's arms. "I was just coming to get some dishes!" she hurriedly explained, reaching for the half-empty cocoa mug.

"You really need to watch what you say on the phone."

"I know."

They remained in a clumsy embrace in the doorway.

Junior was watching his parents with a hopeful expression. "Look!" he said, pointing above their heads. "Mistletoe!"

Trish and Henry glanced up at a bare white wall. Quickly they separated, banging into the doorframe.

"Nice try, hotshot," said Henry, glancing at his watch. "Guess I should prob'ly get back to the office. Big hearing tomorrow."

"Better get going," Junior said bitterly.

"Okay, I'll call you guys tomorrow." Unable to face his younger self another second, Henry fled out the door.

Left in silence, Trish went to comfort her little boy. "Your father still needs to finish the third grade before he can grow up."

"What do you mean? He has a law degree?"

"True, but he lost his soul back on the playground."

"Yeah, well maybe he should check the monkey bars."

"Give 'em a chance; he's trying."

Seven

The sidewalks were crowded with holiday shoppers, not to mention pickpockets, perverts and other forms of degenerates, including one products liability specialist by the name of Henry S. Milton.

Resigned from hustling business, he was merely taking a stroll back to the subway with Mr. Steely. Along the way, he passed a shoeshine boy. Like a character from a Dickens' novel, big eyes peered out from his dirty little face. Taped to his money jar was a crudely printed sign: WILL SHINE SHOES FOR CHRISTMAS MONEY.

"I'll take a shine," said Henry, kicking a brand new Armani up on the boy's stand.

"Hey! Aren't you that jerk-off who sued Santa?"

"You shouldn't be talkin' like that, Tiny Tim."

"That's what my dad calls ya."

"Yeah, well what does your dad do?"

"Construction. Till he broke his back fallin' twenty stories off a building."

Henry winced. "Was there faulty equipment involved?"

"That's what his union's sayin' but my dad says he forgot to fasten his safety belt."

"Has he talked to a lawyer?"

"Nah. He don't believe in suin' people for his own mistakes."

Henry nodded with troubled thoughts. "Wish I could help ya, kid. Sounds like the holidays are gonna be rough on your family."

"We'll get by." The boy concentrated on shining Henry's shoes.

Standing over him, Henry felt an overwhelming shame. From deep inside, an inexplicable warmth came over him. Before he could define it, he was handing over Mr. Steely. "Here, kid. Merry Christmas."

The boy put down his rag to accept the toy. "Hey, this is pretty cool."

"If you push his voice command button, he'll tell you his name."

Sure enough, a battery powered voice came to life: "Hel-lo. My-name-is-Mis-ter Stee-ly."

"Mr. Steely! Alright!" The boy laughed and wound up his new robot toy. Put in motion, Mr. Steely went marching along the curb. The boy followed, ready to catch him should he tumble.

Henry watched them with a glowing smile. "He can also swim in the bathtub. At least that's what the commercial used to promise."

"Don't you have any kids?"

"Yeah, but Junior doesn't want any toys for Christmas."

"What does he want? A trip to Disney World?"

"He wants his jerk-off of a father to come home." Taking a wadded bill from his wallet, Henry dropped it in the boy's jar and headed off.

"Hey! I never finished your shine!"

"Forget about it."

"Yo Henry! You're the coolest jerk-off ever!"

Henry glanced back with a grateful smile, happy to see Mr. Steely with a new best friend.

Eight

Alone in his office, Henry was watching the surveillance video of the Whitfields' home. On a twenty-inch TV, Santa stumbled over the vase and shattered it. Pausing the tape, Henry took a closer look at the treasured piece. Eyes narrowed on the screen, he was oblivious to Nora standing in the doorway.

"Feeling better?" she asked.

Henry looked up at her in surprise. "I dunno. They claim this vase was from the Persian Empire."

"Why not? The Whitfields could buy a museum if they wanted to."

"I'm not so sure about that." Henry opened a file that revealed the Whitfields' assets. "After nine generations of inherited wealth, they may have finally spent the last of their family fortune."

Nora came slinking over to the TV. "That doesn't mean it's a fraud."

"It's awfully shiny for something three-thousand-years-old."

"Maybe they put a protective finish on it."

"I know someone who would know." Henry picked up the phone and dialed a number. After a few rings, a familiar voice answered. "Hey Trish, I was wondering—"

The line was quickly disconnected by Nora.

"What do you think you're doing?"

"My wife is an artist. She would know this kinda stuff."

"Ex-wife and she can only hurt your settlement!"

"But what if it's a fake?"

"Who cares?!"

"That would be a crime."

"You took an oath to best serve your clients."

"I also took an oath to tell the truth, the whole truth and nothing but the truth, so help me God."

"Don't start getting religious on me now, Henry. I didn't invest in you for nothing."

"What am I? Some kind of commodity? A glossy image for one of your ad campaigns?"

"When I first met you, I saw huge potential to build a winner. The Santa Suit gave us that opportunity, and now it's all up to you."

Henry gazed out the window at a hazy Manhattan skyline. "I went to see Junior today. When I left his room, he was looking at me like I was the biggest failure on Earth."

"Boohoo. There're starving kids in Africa and I'm supposed to be moved by that?"

Henry looked at Nora's cover girl face and saw nothing but ugliness. "I think you should leave."

"I'm going to report you to the Bar Association!"

Henry pushed line one for renewed dial tone. "Excuse me, but I need to call my wife. The divorce hasn't been finalized in case you were wondering."

Nora stalked to the doorway, where she turned to glare at Henry with some final words: "I hope you know your feet stink, buster." The door slammed behind her and she was gone from his life.

Before hitting redial, Henry kicked his feet up on the desk to sniff his newly shined shoes. All he smelled was polish, though he was aware enough to realize how unaware we often are of our own imperfections.

Nine

Far more appealing than Henry's shoes, Chinatown smelled of Mongolian beef and savory almond chicken. After meeting his wife and son for a hurried lunch, Henry joined them on a quest for a vase.

"The ancient Persians did make things from soapstone, which turned black and shiny with polishing," said Trish, examining a photo from the Whitfields' file (a minor breech of attorney-client privilege, but who was going to know?)

"So you think it might be genuine?" said Henry.

"Not if we find one down here."

Trish led them past a row of shops selling cheaply manufactured goods. From Oriental rugs to silk blouses to leather handbags, most of these pieces were "Made in Taiwan." Finally they entered an old brick establishment, its namesake in Chinese characters that were flaking off its weathered awning.

* * *

Despite not knowing the name of the place he was entering, Junior happily followed his parents inside. Through a maze of brass and wood furnishings, he was also growing confused. "Dad? Why're you helping Santa now?"

"'Cause I may be the last person in the world who finally believes in 'em."

As they turned down another aisle, Trish made a beeline ahead of them. "Here they are!" She pointed out an entire shelf of vases that were identical to the one in the Whitfields' living room. Lifting one up, she tapped on its ceramic surface. "A step above Kmart, but far from ancient Persia."

"Say cheese," said Henry, taking a proud photo as evidence.

Snooping down the shelf, Junior discovered a price tag. "So Santa only owes them forty bucks?"

"If that was even Santa in the video."

"How can you prove it wasn't?"

"With help from my little youth sleuth," said Henry with a wink.

"You got it!" As Junior followed his parents out of the store, he had a hunch everything would be solved by Christmas.

Ten

Far from heaven in his Pearly Gate Motel room, Santa was reclined on the bed. Puffing on his trademark pipe, at least he didn't have to worry about burning holes in the ratty yellow cover. Decades of cigarette smokers had already made it appear like Swiss cheese.

"That's a funny smellin' tobacco, Mr. Claus," said the rookie elf lawyer.

"It's makin' me hungry," said the chubby elf.

"S'posed to help with arthritis," said Santa. Blowing smoke rings, he flexed his popping knuckles. "Too many winters in the North Pole. I'm more than ready for a sunny beach in paradise. A *real* paradise," he noted, looking at the dripping radiator and television chained to the peeling walls.

Mr. Elfsquire opened a lengthy e-mail on his laptop. "Planet Toys, Inc. is offering a merger from out of this world, but only if you stay on to endorse their products. That would include TV ads and public appearances."

"No. No way! They've already made me out to be the bad guy."

"The people quickly forget, sir. In fact, Planet Toys has already developed a marketing strategy to boost your public image."

"Please consider, Mr. Claus," said the chubby elf. "At least we could still be involved in the toy-making business."

The rest of the elves hopefully nodded.

Santa drew a lengthy puff off his pipe. "Forget about it. I'm ready for Jamaica."

"I'm sorry to hear that, sir," said Mr. Elfsquire.

The elves quietly returned to their computers with saddened little faces.

Eleven

From Chinatown to Broadway in just a matter of blocks, the Miltons discovered Neverland on a brightly lit marquee: PETER PAN THE MUSICAL. Sword drawn, that boy who never wanted to grow up was illuminated in a glossy window poster. Surrounded by singing pirates in tights, he was aided by a glittering Tinkerbell—far leggier as a stage actress than Disney cartoon. Captured in photo instead of glass jar, she still appeared to be in motion, perhaps from a stirring excitement in the air.

"Let's sit in the front row!" said Junior, charging the ticket window.

"Not tonight, kid," said Henry. "We're gonna talk to witnesses."

"Oh, yeah."

"This is better than the show," said Trish. "You get to see your father turn against the pirates."

* * *

Backstage was a dark cavern that might have been mistaken as part of the set. Costumed pirates lumbered about, mumbling lines and using the restroom to relieve pre-performance nerves. Tinkerbell smoked a cigarette as a stagehand fixed her wings. "Yeah, I remember this kid," she said, looking over a photo of Bradley Truffle.

"He was that good?" said Henry, crowding next to Trish and Junior.

"He was that bad. Kid's voice sounded like nails being pulled from a coffin."

"And that was before he swallowed the whistle?"

"Yeah, but who knows what else is stuck in that throat of his? While waiting in the audition room, he gobbled up all the candies, chewed up all the pencils, and almost choked to death on a pen cap."

"Sounds like a stress case."

"Thanks to his showbiz mom. She's the one who pressured him into being here."

"According to her, he's the next Frank Sinatra."

"He'd be lucky to sound like Michael Bolton."

"That's actually what she said."

"In either case, this kid didn't have a prayer. Sad to say, it was his mom's dream, not his." Wings in place, Tinkerbell handed back the photo and fluttered away.

"Thanks Mom and Dad," said Junior, "for not making me put on tights and sing."

Raucous laughter arose from a passing band of pirates.

Henry and Trish joined in with nervous chuckles.

Twelve

Behind the smudged glass was Mr. Bramble, aging superintendent of a rent-by-the-week motel building. Sealed in an airless kiosk, he looked as if he'd spent the past few days in there without a shave, shower or change of clothes. Enraptured by the Knicks game on TV, he munched stale pizza out of a grease-stained box.

"Dat's a foul!" he screamed at the refs. Waving a piece of crust like a switchblade, he reached down his back to scratch inside his T-shirt. Relieved of his itch, he sniffed the flaky crust before sticking it in his mouth with a loud crunch.

"Excuse me," said Henry through the window intercom. "I'm here to see Rene Reno."

Annoyed by the distraction, Mr. Bramble barely glanced over at Henry with his wife and son. "You look familiar. Youz that scumbag bill collector?"

"No, I'm the scumbag lawyer suing Santa Claus, and I really need to talk to her."

"Oh, yeah," said Mr. Bramble with a second glance at Henry. "I seen you on the TV."

Henry smiled. "How 'bout an autograph if you let me in to see her?"

"She don't live here no mores."

Spotting fungi on the lobby couch, Henry didn't look too surprised. "Any idea where she moved to?"

"We ain't exactly pen pals."

"When did she move out?"

"Knowledge don't come cheap here, ya know."

"Mr. Bramble," Henry read from a *Busty Babes* subscription on his desk. "Are you asking me for a bribe?"

"Don't insult me, Mr. Hotshot Lawyer. But now 'dat you brought it up, I could prob'ly use a hundred bucks to help wit' my mutter's operation."

"Sure," Henry reluctantly agreed, reaching into his wallet for a bill that he stuffed through the slot.

Mr. Bramble quickly snatched it up. "She left here yesterday wit' one've 'er men."

"*One* of her men?"

"Guess she wasn't so traumatized by Santa after all," said Trish.

Mr. Bramble banged on the TV for better reception. "She was in such a hurry, she left all 'er crap behind." Through a wave of static, he watched the Knicks forward miss a free throw. "Son of a mother's hemorrhoid! I can't believe dey're payin' 'dis ass munch twenty-million."

"They should trade that ass munch," said Junior.

"Watch your mouth!" said his parents together.

"Damn straight, kid."

"Mind if we look around at her place?"

"For a small donation."

"Fine," said Henry in dismay. "But I haven't made a dime off this case." In a blink of an eye, another Ben Franklin was transformed into a rusty key.

"Room 39-B. Watch out for the mousetrap."

Taking the key, Henry led Trish and Junior to a rickety old elevator.

* * *

Henry stepped in the mousetrap upon entering. "Ouch!" he yelled, kicking the metal device off his foot, only to trip over a pile of dirty clothes.

"It smells like something died in here," said Junior.

"Well it sure wasn't the mouse," said Henry, rubbing a red welt on his ankle.

"She never said her place was a studio," said Trish, glancing over the narrow quarters. A messy queen-size bed took up the majority of the room. Just a few feet away was a miniature fireplace, one that must've been hell on poor Santa's back.

"Santa had no choice but to enter her bedroom," said Henry.

"Where did her kid sleep? The floor?" Junior gazed down on cold hard tiles.

"Let's hope he's staying with his dad," said Henry.

"Then why hang a stocking?" said Junior.

"To bait Santa, why else?" said Trish.

Henry sadly nodded. "Not a single photo of her child anywhere."

"But she's got plenty of her boyfriends on display." Trish opened the closet door to reveal a collage of male strippers.

"Dear Rene," Junior read from a signed photo, "Thanks for last night. You were really hot in—"

Trish tore the photo down before he could finish.

"Let's get outta here," said Henry. "We've seen more than enough."

"Yes, indeed," said Trish with a lusty smile at the stripper's bulge.

"Put that back."

"You can use it as evidence."

Henry snatched the photo and led them out into a dimly lit hallway.

"You're not jealous, are you, Dad?"

"Why would I be?"

"Because he has bigger arms than you."

"Among other things," muttered Trish.

Pretending not to hear, Henry punched the elevator button that had probably stopped lighting up decades ago. "Come on already, I need to get back to the office."

"What about your other clients, Dad? Like that girl who broke her teeth on that jawbreaker?"

"Or that skateboard kid who broke his arm jumping cars?" said Trish.

"What's left to investigate?" said Henry. "It was their own stupidity that got them hurt."

A horrible screeching preceded the elevator doors flapping open.

"Let's take the stairs."

Thirteen

While the city slumbered, a midnight fog silently arose from the Atlantic Ocean and crept over the island of Manhattan. Without warning, it swallowed skyscrapers, apartment buildings, and the Statue of Liberty, her flameless torch left defenseless. Even the moon had been devoured, yet there was one small light that prevailed—the law office window of Henry S. Milton.

Fueled by coffee and adrenaline, Henry rewound the surveillance tape of the Whitfields' home. Half-asleep on his couch were Junior and Trish.

"How many times ya gonna watch that thing, Dad?"

"There's gotta be something on here that proves it's a fraud." Henry pushed play for the umpteenth time.

"You already have the vase," said Trish with a yawn.

"Yeah, but I wanna prove Santa was never there."

"Wait, Dad! Look!"

Henry fumbled to pause the video, freezing Santa in mid-step as he passed the Whitfields' family portraits, including the B-B Twins in matching yellow dresses like two queen bees.

Pointing at the TV, Junior revealed a calendar in the background. "Since when does Santa come in November?" An illustrated turkey could be seen in the monthly display.

"Good question," said Trish, perking up at the screen. "In fact, their cornucopia's still on the table from Thanksgiving dinner—and look how sloppily their tree was put up." Their Christmas tree leaned sideways, its decorations hung haphazardly from untrimmed branches.

"They were obviously in a hurry to set the stage," said Henry. "Right after I filed Bradley's suit."

"Too bad for them," said Trish, "because our little detective's cracked the case."

Junior smiled proudly at his parents. "We did it together."

Fourteen

Beneath the dim glow of his desk lamp, Henry poured through files and letters and complaints, ready to turn them against his clients. Working in the stillness of night, he thought of Benedict Arnold, one of the most despised names in American history. Given his own situation, Henry wondered if Arnold was in fact a traitor, or just a reformed colonial, one who had rebelled against the royal crown, only to later come to his senses. After all, what was a revolution, if not a rowdy gang turning against a higher authority? If so, the rebelling colonials were the traitors, whereas

Arnold was merely a sheep gone astray. Branded by the others for his return to innocence, he would carry their guilt into the future.

Henry shuddered at the thought. Certainly he would lose his law license. That was a given. Plus he would face counter suits from his clients, likely to exceed his malpractice premiums. Worse yet, his insurance company would probably fight his claim with their own team of lawyers. That would mean bankruptcy, loss of career, no means of feeding his family or himself.

As the first rays of dawn seeped through the window, he watched his wife and son asleep on the couch. Surely they'd forgive him if he changed his mind at the last minute. Or would they? Henry sighed and rubbed his burning eyes. Standing from his chair, he went to the window to watch the sunrise. Through a morning haze, the Statue of Liberty stood resilient against fierce winds, her knees unbuckled by the waves crashing against her.

"Nine billion dollars," he whispered to himself. That was the rumored settlement offer according to the newspapers. "Nine billion," he repeated, and one-third of that would be his, once Santa liquidated his North Pole toy factory.

With three billion dollars, Henry could barely imagine where to start spending it. A mansion in Long Island perhaps, with a fourteen-car garage filled with exotic cars. Jaguar, Ferrari, Maserati, Mercedes, Lamborghini...

Cruising in style, he and Junior would return to the Bronx for Yankees games. In fact, they could buy the Yankees if they ever went up for sale. Imagine that! Henry the owner, Junior vice-president and GM. What a pair they'd make!

As for Trish, she could open her own art studio right in the heart of New York. Maybe one in Paris, London, Prague, wherever she wanted. Knowing Trish, she would probably sponsor other artists, hosting exhibits to display their works. A prestigious endowment could be founded in her name. The Trish P. Milton Award for Starving Artists. Something like that.

What a life he could give them.

"Hey Dad," came Junior's sleepy voice from the couch. "I'm really glad you're helping Santa."

Henry turned from the window to face his son.

"Me too," he said without a trace of doubt.

Fifteen

Normally a settlement hearing would've taken place in a conference room; but with the recent invasion of media cameras, Judge Thorne had no choice but to schedule it in his courtroom. No longer filling the role of judge, the former naval commander was now a presiding mediator.

With Santa's surrender declared, the war was over, yet the waters remained turbulent. Aside from Henry's clients in attendance were thousands of others who had filed claims via certified mail. It could take weeks, if not months, to sort through them, determining how much, if anything, each plaintiff would receive.

"Let's get started with the proceeding," said Judge Thorne, hammering his gavel to silence the noisy courtroom.

"Your Honor," said Henry, approaching the bench. "I'd like to begin with a further review of the tape."

"How many times must he drag me through the mud?" Santa complained to his elf lawyers. Disgustedly they watched Henry insert the tape for viewing.

"Can you see the screen, Mr. Claus?"

Santa squinted at the TV through his little round spectacles. "I must've forgotten my glasses again," he said, patting his pockets in frustration. "Where'd I put those darn things?"

"You're wearing them," said Judge Thorne.

"Perhaps you need a new prescription," said Mr. Elfsquire.

"Actually," said Henry, "I believe he's wearing Mr. Whitfield's glasses."

A curious buzz arose from the audience in which the Whitfields exchanged nervous glances.

"I don't understand," said Judge Thorne.

"I believe the Whitfields planted those glasses," said Henry. "Just like they planted this vase." A replay on TV showed Santa stumbling over the so-called relic of the Persian Empire. "In case you haven't finished your Christmas shopping, your Honor, you may find one on sale for forty dollars." To everyone's surprise, Henry presented the photo of the vases in the Chinatown shop.

"Mr. Milton," said Judge Thorne over a stir of excitement in the room. "You realize what you're doing here could cost you your license to practice law?"

"Not to mention a secure future for my family. Plus a mansion in Long Island and ownership of the Yankees."

"I see you've put some thought into this?"

"Yes, your Honor."

Trish and Junior smiled proudly in the front row. Privy to his next move, they watched Henry fast-forward the tape to its digitally-marked spot.

"Mr. and Mrs. Whitfield. Do you regularly change the months of your calendar?"

"Of course we do!"

"We're responsible people with busy schedules!"

"That's right," said the B-B Twins in snotty voices.

"Yes," said Henry, pointing to a frozen image on the TV. "I can see that November was a busy month for your family." On a much larger screen than the one in his office, the turkey was brightly displayed on the calendar photo.

The audience gasped in surprise.

"I'd have to be getting really senile to go flying on the wrong holiday," said Santa.

"Not a chance," said Mr. Elfsquire. "In fact, our computers show the B-B Twins were on your naughty list last year."

"Which means you never entered the house at all," said the rookie elf.

"We finished our investigation last night," said the chubby elf. "But all you could talk about was Jamaica."

"Why were they on your naughty list?" asked Judge Thorne.

"For tricking a first grader into licking a frozen pole," Santa read from Mr. Elfsquire's report.

"She was dumb enough to fall for it!" protested the B-B Twins.

"But this courtroom is smarter than that," said Henry.

"What about me?" said Shelly Sheepshank. "I really did break my teeth!"

"Pain and suffering!" claimed Max Wheeler, waving his arm cast for all to see. "Santa owes us!"

"I was first!" whistled Bradley. "I deserve the most!"

Rene Reno stood in a leggy miniskirt. "Santa *was* my first! He robbed me of my innocence!"

"Don't you have a child?" inquired Judge Thorne with a raised eyebrow.

"Not that she remembers to call on his birthday," said Henry, resisting the temptation to peek down her cleavage on live TV. "Miss Reno? How's the new boyfriend working out?"

"Why, I told you! Thanks to Santa, I'm too emotionally damaged to have a significant other!"

Several male strippers jumped to their feet in the audience. In street clothes, they looked much different than their photos in Rene's closet.

"Then what am I?"

"Or me?"

"You said I was your boyfriend!"

"You promised me a trip to Hawaii!"

"Me too! After you settled this case, you cheating ho!"

"Ho-ho-ho!" chuckled Santa.

"I've never even seen these men before!" insisted Rene Reno.

"Oh, really? Then what were they doing on your wall?" Henry opened his briefcase for the signed photo.

"You had no right going into my room!" shrieked Rene.

"Collecting evidence," said Henry. He winked at Trish before handing the racy photo to Judge Thorne.

"Reminds me of Seaman Davy in his skivvies," said his Honor with a smile before quickly filing it away. "Are we almost done here, Mr. Milton?"

"Just about." Turning to Bradley, Henry said: "You never wanted to be in showbiz, did you, kid?"

Bradley nervously chewed on his fingernails. "And how would you know?"

"Let's just say I talked to Tinkerbell."

"How dare you!" said Mrs. Truffle.

"You might try therapy for you and your son, Mrs. Truffle. Before he chews off his fingers and chokes to death on them."

Bradley gagged on a fingernail.

"Stop that right now!" said his mother, dragging him out of the courtroom. "We're gonna go find another lawyer!"

"Good riddance," said Henry, before confronting his last two clients: Shelly Sheepshank and Max Wheeler. "Under English common law, you two should've practiced common sense. Meaning you don't bite into a jawbreaker or play stuntman on a flimsy skateboard."

The two kids whined in protest.

"Let's go," said Mr. Sheepshank, leading his daughter out of the courtroom.

The other clients followed like a wounded pack of wolves.

"Wait for me!" cried Rene Reno, trying to keep up in stiletto heels.

"Case dismissed," declared Judge Thorne, hammering his gavel with supreme authority.

A jubilant cheer erupted from the audience.

"We did it, Dad!"

"We sure did!" Henry joined his family in celebration.

"Your Honor!" said Mr. Elfsquire. "Does this mean all charges have been dropped against my client?"

"I'm going to call the prosecutor's office now." Judge Thorne retreated into his chambers.

"Ho-ho-ho!" bellowed Santa. "So much for retirement. Mrs. Claus will just have to wait for that topless beach in paradise."

The elves cringed at the thought.

"I'd much rather see Miss Brazil," said Mr. Elfsquire, as Santa wandered off into a throng of reporters.

"I wonder if she dates shorter men," said the plum-haired elf, instantly blushing purple.

"Or younger ones," said the rookie elf.

"Or chubby ones," said the chubby elf.

"I think she'd prefer an older, wiser man," said Mr. Elfsquire, which started a heated debate among lawyers. As they argued over a woman they would never meet, Santa found Henry in the festive crowd.

"I'm proud of you, Henry."

Henry smiled like a little boy. "Thank you, Santa."

"And you only have to do one more thing to get off my naughty list for good."

"What's that?"

"You said it best. Common sense." Santa winked at Trish and Junior before heading back to his bickering elves.

Henry slowly nodded at Santa's advice. Facing his wife and son, he pleaded: "I know I've been an idiot husband and father, but you guys mean the world to me, and all I want for Christmas is to go home with my family."

Due to the chaotic noise in the courtroom, Henry could not hear Trish's answer—but judging by her kiss on his mouth, her body in his arms, he would have to presume that was a yes.

Sixteen

On the courthouse steps was another media flurry, reporters fighting for position like pigeons feeding off a popcorn-covered sidewalk. Amidst the confusion were America's two favorite TV personalities:

"Live from the federal superior courthouse in New York, I'm Carol Patrick," said Patrick Carol.

"And I'm Patrick Carol," said Carol Patrick.

Quickly realizing their mix-up, they reported together: "Bringing you a shocking turnaround."

"As Santa wins back the hearts of New Yorkers."

"And boys and girls across the world."

"Proven by the thousands among us now, awaiting Mr. Claus to appear through these very front doors."

Swarms of people returned with signs: SORRY, SANTA! They packed the streets, leaned from windows and balconies, and even climbed up poles for a glimpse of their resurrected hero.

"I don't know about you, Carol, but I'm still a bit numbed by Henry Milton's sudden change of—"

"Wait! Here he comes now!"

Henry exited the courthouse with his wife and son. Through the tangle of microphones and reporters, they could barely move.

"Henry!" Carol shouted. "How does it feel to be giving up billions of dollars?"

Henry smiled into the bright lights of the news cameras. "Better than I ever could've imagined."

"In anticipation of your law license being revoked," said Patrick, "What are you planning for your future?"

"What really matters is today. And after taking a family vote, we've decided on pizza and a movie."

"Sodas and ice cream too, Dad!"

"Sure thing, kid." Henry joyfully led his family down the steps.

The crowd greeted them with deafening cheers.

"Way to go, Henry!" several voices screamed.

Standing tall like a king at five-feet-eight, Henry smiled and waved to the loving masses. With his queen and young prince by his side, he floated downward as if in a fairy tale.

Seventeen

WELCOME HOME, YOU LUCKY BASTARD!

Instead of such a banner were three stockings hung over the fireplace. One for Henry, Trish, and Junior, their names appearing in red felt letters over fuzzy white trim. As part of an arts and crafts project led by Trish, they had cut them out and pasted them on the night before.

Now, in the wee hours of morning, the first rays of daylight peeked through the curtains. The weatherwoman had called for a gray Christmas, meaning fog, drizzle, and overcast. But this year, Henry was grateful to have a roof over his head to protect him from what he used to see as bad omens. And speaking of weather, a thunder of footsteps suddenly shook the house. Storming down the hallway, the Miltons appeared in pajamas and messy hair, their teeth unbrushed.

O' to be alive as they tore through their stockings!

"A Gameboy!"

"A new watch!"

"Paint brushes!"

"Baseball cards!"

Junior ripped open the package and thumbed through a series of Mets players. "Dad? These must be from Santa?"

"Sorry, son. They were all outta the Yankees." Henry held up a pair of odor eaters for his shoes. "These must be from you guys."

"Actually, Dad. They're for us more than you."

Joining in the laughter, Henry plundered through his stocking like a kid in the third grade. "Cologne and deodorant too. Guess I'll be smelling good this year." To Henry's surprise, he discovered an old friend nestled in Hershey's kisses. "Mr. Steely? How'd Santa know I gave 'em away?"

"We found him on eBay," said Trish. "Some guy in Renton, Washington had one that was never taken from the box."

"Wow! Thanks." Henry wound up his robot and sent him marching. A snag in the carpet made him tumble face first. "Mr. Steely needs to stay outta the eggnog."

Laughter filled the Miltons' living room.

"Hey Mom! What else did Santa get you?" Junior gave his father a knowing smile as Trish reached into her stocking for a jewelry box. Face aglow, she opened it to see a sparkling diamond necklace.

"Oh Henry!"

Henry gently brushed the wisps of hair from her neck to help clasp it on. "That looks beautiful on you. Even in pajamas."

"Yeah, Mom. You look hot."

Trish smiled at her reflection in the fireplace glass. "Thank you so much. But I really don't think we can afford this right now. My artworks aren't exactly selling like hotcakes." Crowding the shelf were her sculptures, including the angel watching over them.

"I'll find another job," said Henry. "I'd be good at selling used cars."

"Please no," said Junior and Trish together.

"Then what am I gonna do?"

A troubled silence filled the room. As they searched for answers, something glimmered from the bottom of Henry's stocking.

"What's that, Dad?"

Henry fished out a silvery envelope. "Is this from you guys?"

Trish and Junior curiously shook their heads no.

Henry opened it to read over a letter. "Santa's offering me a job—as a liability specialist to prevent future lawsuits—while ensuring the good boys and girls receive their toys."

"That's wonderful, Henry!"

"Does this mean we're moving to the North Pole, Dad?"

"It doesn't say."

"That's okay," said Junior, pulling them into a hug. "So long as we're all together."

"That's right," his parents happily agreed.

"Oh, look!" said Junior, pointing above them. "Mistletoe!" He dashed off with his stocking to leave his parents alone.

"He's not joking this time," said Henry. Directly overhead was a fresh cut of mistletoe that Junior must've placed there.

"Well," said Trish. "We wouldn't want to break tradition."

"Oh, no, that might upset Santa."

Lips meeting in a kiss, they wished each other a very merry Christmas.

Eighteen

Of course it was dark at the North Pole, where the top of the earth faced darkness through most of winter. But even in darkness came light, with fireflies sprinkling the air like electric snowflakes. Imported from the American South, where rhythm and blues was born, they now inhabited the heated deck of Santa's home, sweet, home.

The mesh gate swung open and Santa traipsed in, his face, beard and clothing blackened with soot.

"How'd it go?" said Mrs. Claus from her rocking chair facing the sky.

"My back's a little stiff, but I can't complain." Taking a seat next to his wife, he sipped from a steaming mug of cocoa that awaited him on a stand. "Mmmm, that's delicious, Mrs. Claus."

"You earned it, Pops."

As they sat in peaceful silence, all they heard were the gentle creaks of floorboards beneath their rocking chairs.

"This was a tough year," said Santa, taking off his filthy mitten to hold her hand.

"Yes, but let's not forget. We've survived two world wars and the Great Depression, not to mention countless decades of marriage."

"Yes, indeed." Santa sipped his cocoa and stared off into space.

"What's the matter, Pops?"

"Oh. Nothing." Rocking back and forth in his chair, Santa kept rhythm with a song in his head: "I Want You, I Need You, I Love You." So many years ago, he and Mrs. Claus had slow danced to that tune on a warm summer night.

"Is it Elvis?" Mrs. Claus was able to read his thoughts after all their time together.

"Yes," he softly replied.

With a slight nod, Mrs. Claus reached into her shawl for a Parcels-Express envelope advertising: FASTER THAN SANTA ACROSS THE WORLD. "This came for you today. It's from New York."

Santa turned it over to see a return address from Henry Milton, Junior. Tearing it open, he read aloud: "Dear Santa. Thank you for giving my dad a job. He really needs it."

"Darling boy," said Mrs. Claus with a smile. "What else does it say?"

Santa cleared his throat before continuing: "P.S. You may not be God or Cupid, but you still brought a miracle. My dad came home and he's kissing my mom beneath the mistletoe."

Santa folded the letter and put it back in its envelope.

"You're a good man," his wife gently reminded him.

"But I'm sure no saint. Not a real one anyway."

"Maybe not, but I never believed a single word those tabloids wrote about you."

"Why should you? Rene Reno isn't half the woman you are."

"Oh, you silly old man. You truly are going blind."

They chuckled in the night, their cloudy breaths stirring the air. Without warning, the fireflies scattered up, up and away into the sky.

"They sure took off in a hurry," said Santa, as they watched them blend perfectly into the stars.

"Must be the magnetic pull of the universe."

"Yes," Santa realized. "There's an invisible hand at work."

"That's right, Pops, and you can only do so much."

Santa nodded while gazing upwards. From planet Earth, one might have seen anything in that great constellation of connecting dots. A five-year-old girl might have seen Frosty the Snowman, all decked out in top hat, scarf and pipe. A high school boy might have seen Miss Brazil in all her glorious curves. Through Santa's eyes appeared Elvis Presley. Eternally young, his stars burning bright, Elvis performed "Silent Night" for anyone in the galaxy who wanted to see.

"Merry Christmas, sweetheart."

"You too, Pops."

The cover wreath was designed by Angela Dawn Perry.

As co-founder of Fat Nose Illustration with Thomas William Perry (a.k.a. "Pez") she used photos, paintings and clay sculptures that were digitally scanned and edited. Based in Peterborough, UK, Fat Nose offers services worldwide. Write to: fat_nose_illustration@hotmail.co.uk